Tcke

LOSING IS WHAT MATTERS

MANUEL PÉREZ SUBIRANA

LOSING IS WHAT MATTERS

A NOVEL

TRANSLATED BY ALLEN YOUNG

DALKEY ARCHIVE PRESS

Originally published in Spanish as *Lo importante es perder* in 2003.

© 2003 by Manuel Pérez Subirana
Translation copyright © 2016 by Allen Young

First edition, 2016
All rights reserved

Library of Congress Cataloging-in-Publication Data

Names: Pérez Subirana, Manuel, 1971- author. | Young, Allen, 1978-
translator.
Title: Losing is what matters / by Manuel Pérez Subirana ; translated by
Allen Young.
Other titles: *Lo importante es perder*. English
Description: First edition. | Victoria, TX : Dalkey Archive Press, 2016.
Identifiers: LCCN 2015040722 | ISBN 9781564788665 (pbk. : acid-free paper)
Classification: LCC PQ6716.E473 L6513 2016 | DDC 863/.7--dc23
LC record available at http://lccn.loc.gov/2015040722

Partially funded by the Illinois Arts Council, a state agency.

 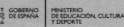

This work has been published with a subsidy from the Ministry of Education,
Culture and Sport of Spain.

www.dalkeyarchive.com
Victoria, TX / McLean, IL / Dublin

Dalkey Archive Press publications are, in part, made possible through the support of
the University of Houston-Victoria and its program in creative writing, publishing,
and translation.

Printed on permanent/durable acid-free paper

LOSING IS WHAT MATTERS

1

It's NOT NICE to be dumped, to be left by the woman you've lived with for more than three years, to be phoned by her at the office one afternoon and told in a voice that trembles more than usual that you urgently need to talk, and then gamely, full of goodwill, to cancel all your appointments and meet the woman half an hour later on the patio of some bar, intrigued but at a loss, not suspecting what's about to happen, not even knowing whether what you're about to hear is good news or bad news, or good and bad at the same time, and then to arrive at the bar and sit down with a gin and tonic that you ordered heavy on the gin, just in case, and to see the woman appear, to study her face and know then that any chance of good news is out of the question, to see the woman you've been living with for more than three years greet you coldly, without the usual kiss, sit down, cross her legs and start to talk, to hear from her mouth words you've heard too many times on television, in plays, in movies, words read in novels, reeled off in unoriginal dreams, sung in popular songs, words so familiar and so clichéd that you hear them like a tedious, irritating hum, words like "we could use a break," or "things between us have changed," or "we can still be good friends," or "it had to end sooner or later." It's not nice.

No, it's not nice to get dumped. And yet you don't always start to cry or feel your heart skip a beat, or cough in surprise on the gin and tonic you ordered heavy on the gin, just in case. You don't always grasp, in that first moment, that the shared world which sheltered you for more than three years has begun to crumble, and from that very instant each and every one of the ingredients of your life in common has already begun to disintegrate: words, landscapes, meals, glances, fragrances, budgets, future plans, schedules, memories; you don't always understand then that from this moment on you're no longer quite the person you were, you've started to become someone else, something else, another project. No, it may not be nice, but the world doesn't always collapse in these situations. News of a certain momentousness, the kind that determines the future and rearranges the past, can't find a proper place in the present, in our present. We need time to pass so that we can confirm for ourselves, on the ground, like meticulous scientists of our own existence, that what we were told, inconceivable as it seemed at the time, has in fact come to pass, has unfurled all its ramifications irreparably over our lives. Because the present gives no credence to momentous news, especially news that can hurt us. In order for us to grasp and assimilate what we've just heard, we would need everything around us to pause and join us in our surprise and our bewilderment. But time doesn't pause, and all things continue on their course, and the waitress who brought us the gin and tonic is still moving about the patio, oblivious to the news we've just received, with a tray in one hand and the same miniskirt that unsettled us when we first arrived at the bar, and while the woman at the table repeats for the third time that "the passion is over between us," you surprise yourself tilting your head trying to see if you can take in another inch of the waitress's legs; and meanwhile a motorcycle roars down the avenue while you think, still watching the waitress and listening to the woman you've lived with for more than three years, that life in the city is getting worse by the day, and that they should really crack down on those reckless bikers. And what about that little rock that got into your shoe when you headed to meet her and which you haven't had the time or the energy to remove? Yes, it's still there, stuck to your big toe, and you move your foot nervously, ineffectually, trying to make it at least change position while you hear you're being dumped, it's over, c'est fini; and so many other pointless, minor details that you'll forget a few seconds later but which at this moment, trying to find a foothold inside you, compete with the news that will change your life.

I remember a man, a good person I'm sure, who was at the

neighborhood bar playing cards with his friends one day when someone burst in to tell him his wife had just been struck by a car and killed. The man, not taking his eyes off his cards, waved his free hand in the direction of the bearer of bad news and shot back, "Later, tell her I can't right now, not now, for Christ's sake, not now." No doubt one expects these things to happen some other way. It's not possible for your wife to be struck by a car when you're in the bar with friends and four aces burning in your left hand. "Not now, for Christ's sake, not now," said the man. And with good reason: momentous news is incompatible with the present. It needs time. We need time. I must have thought the same thing as I watched the woman who until then had been my wife walk away, with that air of timid solemnity that clings to those who leave us. Later, my love, I'll suffer later. And I ordered another gin and tonic from the waitress, and I remembered I'd canceled all my appointments and had the rest of the day free, and I told myself that, all things considered, the afternoon wasn't shaping up to be so bad.

Now that I know what happened later, in the following weeks, I can only feel ridiculous and loathsome for that first reaction, but I should confess that later that day, after being left by the woman I once loved and perhaps still loved, I felt as though a web of possibilities that I had been denied ever since I began going out with Elisenda now opened up again majestically before me. And I confess I felt a happy and irresponsible freedom, and I admit I smoked three cigarettes with intense pleasure, one with dark-leaf tobacco, as I savored my second gin and tonic and looked out, carefree and amused, at the bustle of the street.

2

I MET ALBERTO Cisnerroso at the university, halfway through my second year, though I noticed him around long before that. I saw him for the first time a few days after I arrived on campus, in the café, drinking a glass of red wine and smoking a thin cigar as he paged through the newspaper *El País*. That's how I must have seen him during my first year, practically every day, in the same spot, almost always sitting at the same table. I'd catch a glimpse of him, cast a furtive glance toward where he sat as I hurried anxiously through the café toward the first-year classrooms, with that undignified and humiliating insecurity of someone who still isn't on familiar ground and finds everything hostile and threatening.

His preposterous habits, his outlandishly elegant clothes, his haughty and exaggerated manner, his chumminess with the staff, the fact that I never saw him in class all made me assume he wasn't a first-year. Later on, however, after I got to know some of my classmates, one of whom had crossed paths with him at enrollment, I learned that I was mistaken, that the student who spent his mornings in the café drinking red wine and smoking cigars while the rest of us sat consumed by boredom in the lecture halls was a newbie like me. I also learned that no one had seen him attend class, and no one had seen him speak to anyone other than the waitstaff or one of the oddballs who occasionally came to visit him at the café and weren't law students, judging by appearances. I learned all this, and also learned my classmates didn't like him and thought him pompous and conceited. For that matter, I didn't have a much higher opinion of him. His dismissive, smug attitude annoyed me, as did his way of looking down his nose at anyone who walked by. And still, even though this opinion was my own and I often joined in when my classmates talked bad about him, something about Alberto secretly attracted me.

I ended up studying law more out of certain family pressures and the inertia of youth than out of any real interest in the field. Even so, I harbored quite a few expectations for university life. Weary of my friends from high school, eager to meet new people, impatient to test out my recently acquired independence, I saw the university as the starting point for a new life, the alluring space that would fulfill my life's ambitions and transform me into something special.

It didn't take me long to realize how mistaken I was. The university was in no way what I'd been led to believe by things I had read or heard from my older acquaintances. The dreary atmosphere quickly dragged me down into a sadness and boredom that I found nearly intolerable. My classmates, who I imagined would be extraordinarily interesting people, turned out to be well-behaved, disciplined young men and women who hurried down the halls to make their next class and whose conversation rarely strayed beyond the purely academic. I felt cheated and alone, and it pained me to think of the five years that lay ahead of me.

The first year ended and the second began. Nothing changed. Not even my attempts to take a certain interest in the law bore fruit. I studied just enough to pass my exams, and I attended class and took notes mechanically. I continued to see Alberto around. He hadn't changed his habits, either. He still spent his mornings in the café and seemed not to have made any friends at school. I didn't know whether he had also passed his first year, though I doubted it.

One day in February, shortly before midterms, I went to campus and waited a quarter of an hour for the Civil Law professor to show up, only to be told by a secretary that class was canceled. Exams were coming up and most of the students went to the library to study. That was my plan, too, but since I stayed behind to photocopy some Commercial Law notes that a classmate had lent me, by the time I reached the library all the seats were taken. I thought about going to the courtyard, which had some benches, but spring hadn't quite arrived and the cold dissuaded me. In the end I elected to go to the café. There were some students having breakfast there, including three or four from my year, but I didn't know them well enough to sit down at their table, nor am I the kind of person who likes to talk to strangers. I looked in a corner of the café, near the doors that opened onto the courtyard. Alberto wasn't there, and the table he usually occupied was free. Normally, when I reached campus, he was already in the café reading the newspaper, but sometimes, presumably when he overslept, he'd arrive later and I'd see him only after classes ended, as I walked through the café on my way home. "He must have overslept today," I thought, and even though there were more than a few unoccupied tables, once I'd gotten my café au lait, I decided to sit where Alberto usually sat.

I began to flip through the Commercial Law notes, but I could barely make out my classmate's writing. I held the page a few inches from my face and then moved it away from my eyes again, but nothing I read made any sense. After several minutes struggling with that infernal handwriting, I suddenly felt someone watching me. I must have noticed a shadow fall across the paper in front of my eyes.

I looked up and saw Alberto Cisnerroso standing before me, a glass of red wine in each hand. His eyebrows were raised, and his upper lip was perched on his lower one, but I could make out the beginnings of a smile. We stared at each other for a few seconds in silence. "Looks like we'll have to share a table," said Alberto at last. He slid a chair over with his foot and sat down, placing the glasses on the table in such a way that one of them ended up next to my coffee. And then I don't know what came over me, I don't know what made me assume Alberto had brought that glass of wine for me; perhaps it just seemed inconceivable that someone could drink two glasses of red wine at nine thirty in the morning in the campus café, but in any event, not wanting to seem rude, I grabbed the closer glass, full of wine I not only didn't want but which, at that time of day, immediately after my coffee, I found rather nauseating. "Thanks a lot," I said, forcing a smile and bringing the glass up to my lips. Then, since I hadn't stopped looking at him, I saw Alberto raise his eyebrows even higher, part his lips and hold his mouth open while I sipped, timidly, a tiny amount of the wine. Seeing his face, it dawned on me that I had made a mistake: the glass was not intended for me. It dawned on me, and as it did I began to blush, that at no time had Alberto meant to offer me that wine. I brought the glass down quickly from my lips and set it on the table, looking at the individual now sitting across from me. I remained silent, red with embarrassment at the situation and disgust at the liquid traveling at that very moment down my throat. The expression on my face must have moved him to pity; with a benevolent smile he wiped the confusion off his face and put out his hand. "Alberto Cisnerroso," he said, introducing himself. We shook, and forcing back a gag, I told him my name.

Alberto Cisnerroso was drunk. He slurred his speech and had trouble focusing his eyes on a single point. He told me he'd had a rough night (his words) and still hadn't made it to bed. Later on I learned that, to fight hangovers, Alberto had acquired the habit (a habit I too eventually acquired) of drinking two glasses of red wine or, failing that, two small glasses of beer, but that morning, no doubt to ease my embarrassment, he not only didn't mention this fact, but also compelled me to finish the wine by insisting that he had, of course, ordered it for me.

Alberto spoke without looking at me, as if I weren't there. I barely remember his words, partly because of the nervousness that came over me and partly because it was actually difficult to understand what he was saying. I know he offered me a cigar, and I refused, pointing to the cigarette I held between my fingers. I remember having seen two classmates of mine with whom I had become somewhat friendly on their way to the next class. They looked at me in surprise and one of them shook his head. "What on earth are you doing with him?" he seemed to ask. I waved discreetly. Then I looked at my watch: it was five after ten; I had Administrative Law. Alberto must have noticed me looking, because he lifted his head and asked if I had class. I hesitated for a minute and finally replied that no, I had the next period free. He shrugged. When he stopped talking, I pretended to read the Commercial Law notes I had in my lap, as though justifying my continued presence there, across from him, at his table. The minutes went by. Alberto looked agitated, he kept glancing at the bar, probably pondering whether or not to order a second glass of wine, the glass I'd so clumsily taken from him. He also inspected the other tables looking for something or someone. "You don't happen to have *El País*, do you?" he asked, eyes half-closed. I said I didn't, but most likely he wasn't listening. Immediately thereafter he looked up at the clock on the wall, rubbed his face, got up, and left the table without saying good-bye.

"Stupid bastard," I thought, watching his slim, compact figure walk out of the café. Seeing him then, hair combed, blazer sitting perfectly on his shoulders, silk shirt tucked into his corduroy pants, ascot tied perfectly around his neck, no one would think he was drunk and hadn't yet made it to bed. As he walked by the bar, the waiter greeted him effusively, and Alberto, hardly looking at him, raised a hand to acknowledge the greeting and continued on his way.

"Stupid bastard," I repeated to myself. But one can't always control what one feels, and it's not always easy to make our opinions, which are often straightforward and unequivocal, like thinking *this guy's a total ass*, match up with what, involuntarily, even against our better judgment, we've begun to feel. Someone seems interesting or likeable for reasons beyond rational comprehension that we can't quite put our finger on, and even though the most overt and conspicuous part of that individual leads us to think the opposite, that he's an idiot or an awful person, we find ourselves unable to use this information to align our feelings with common sense. In the same way, we fall in love with a woman we know to be stuck-up or hysterical, and when our friends, in a moment of frankness, ask what we're doing with a woman like that, we reply that we can't help it. I didn't lie when, talking with my classmates and concurring with their opinions, I said I thought Alberto was a pompous show-off, nor did I misrepresent my thoughts that morning by repeating, as I watched him walk away, that he was a stupid bastard. No, that was precisely what I thought. And yet, at the same time, I felt sorry he had left, and I wondered, somewhat anxiously, whether I'd ever have the chance to talk to him again.

I looked at my watch. The Administrative Law professor had probably arrived at the classroom by now. In any case, I didn't feel like attending class, nor did I want to continue to wrestle with the Commercial Law notes. I left campus and started to walk. I spent all morning strolling along the Avenida del Diagonal.

In youth, solitude is hard to bear. Perhaps later, with age, we discover certain pleasures in being alone, and even at times feel the need to get away from others to take stock of where we are and what has become of our life. But in youth, when our whole future lies ahead of us, when we still haven't fully discovered those traits that will let others recognize us and match us to a distinct personality, or let us do the same, solitude appears as a hindrance to life, an obstacle stemming the flow of our vitality, a bleak, forbidding dam holding back the rushing desire to find, through others, an extension of ourselves that can eventually materialize in something beyond our own abstractions.

I disliked this Alberto character, who seemed to look down on everyone else from on high, yet from the very beginning, deep down, part of me acted as though he were my only connection to the idealized image of college life that I'd formed, the only one who could pull me out of the labyrinth of solitude in which I felt trapped.

The day after that ludicrous encounter, as I passed by the café early in the morning, I heard someone calling out my name. I didn't quite react at first, and my feet, carrying me at a brisk pace toward the classrooms, even continued a few steps before slowing to a stop. Then I turned around and saw Alberto waving at me, silently now, hand in the air, smiling and leaning slightly to one side.

They're strange, those times when the seconds seem to slow their pace and join us in our indecision, waiting attentively for us to take a step in one direction or another, to acknowledge the greeting briefly and politely, for example, and continue on our way, or instead to set aside our hesitation and walk three or four yards out of our way to the table and say a more extended hello, extended enough for our acquaintance to invite us to join him, and in joining him enter a world of new possibilities; confusing, tense moments when what we do, what we ultimately choose to do, will rarely follow from a logical or reasoned decision; we will act (and depending on what we do, perhaps nothing will ever be the same) according to our whims.

Everything changed after that morning, after the moment when an irrational instinct led me to approach Alberto's table and return his greeting in a drawn-out and friendly enough fashion that he decided to ask me to sit down for a minute at his table. Everything began to change at that point, even though later, with the certainty and pride of someone who has achieved his goals, I credited the force of destiny, and not simply a gratuitous, random whim, with saving me from the tedium I had sunk into. Because when the changes you wished for finally come, the changes and events you've pursued for years, you welcome them as something natural and unsurprising, as if they were inevitably destined for you, as if you'd always known for certain they would arrive. And you forget then about the hardships along the way, about all the times you were about to give up and throw in the towel. The politician who becomes a minister thinks his whole life has led up to his appointment to the post; and the singer catapulted to stardom overnight loses sight of the threat of failure, claiming to have always been convinced she'd make it; and the man who at last, after pursuing a woman for more than ten years, receives the first exquisite, redeeming kiss, declares without a blush that he never doubted such a moment would come. So too I felt that my friendship with Alberto was the work of fate and therefore inevitable, and right away I found it perfectly natural that I should spend my mornings with him in the café, stop going to class, break off the few friendships I'd made during my first year, and adopt as instinctive, as my own, behaviors and attitudes I had previously derided as idiotic. The

long months of powerlessness and despair, the endless days of
loneliness and boredom I had endured with such difficulty before
I met Alberto, would remain stored in my memory like a slight,
insignificant episode, like an unnecessary bureaucratic delay.

Of the three years that followed (the three years my friendship
with Alberto lasted), I retain, aside from a chronic bronchitis, a
hazy, contradictory nostalgia—hazy and contradictory because,
while I'm now wholly aware of how much we were playing artificial, made-up roles, and therefore how pathetic we were (especially in my case, since I lacked my friend's genius and wit), it's
also true that even in the balanced judgment of hindsight those
were happy days, perhaps the only truly happy days I've ever
known in my life.

Nostalgia and embarrassment mingle now, for instance,
when I recall the many mornings I spent with Alberto in the
campus café, the endless hours we whiled away arrogantly
watching young men and women hurry past us with their law
books and binders. Lazy, slow mornings, proudly and mili-
tantly unproductive, once in a while broken up by a visit from
one of Alberto's friends, outlandish characters I'd seen since
my first year and who I eventually discovered were mostly
history students, although there was also no shortage of hard-
to-place individuals whom not even Alberto seemed to know
very much about and who claimed some sort of always unde-
monstrated artistic talent. When there were visitors, Alberto
assumed the role of master of ceremonies, sitting at the head
of the rectangular table and leading the group in a sparkling,
laughing banter that never went flat. More than a few times,
after several beers and glasses of wine and coffee spiked with
Marie Brizard, the café's usual calm gave way to a commotion and a chaos which the reserved law students regarded
sternly with disapproval, but which the waiters, all of them
good friends of Alberto, pretended not to notice.

Slowly, and not without a certain pride and satisfaction, I

came to believe that I, too, gained the reputation for extrava-
gance and mischief that Alberto had enjoyed since first year.
I stopped talking to the people who until then had been my
friends, and I read their wary, frowning expressions as an
unmistakable sign of envy and secret admiration.

Still, even though we were always together and behaved
in a similar fashion, Alberto clearly took the lead, and could
claim responsibility for the reputation we gained on campus.
I did little more, in fact, than follow in his footsteps and model
my persona on the pattern he provided. I should make clear
that none of this made me feel less important, or like a background character. Only in the eyes of others does a follower
have an inferior status; he takes pride in his rank and considers
it a privilege, since he thinks, quite wrongly, that some of the
leader's light lends a shine to his own figure. In this way homely
girls latch on to the prettier ones, believing beauty to be contagious at close range. Neither the follower nor the homely girl,
nor myself at that time, dazzled as I was by Alberto, realize
that a disciple's personality is always eclipsed by the leader's,
and that finishing second is worse than bringing up the rear. I
didn't realize this, and had someone tried to tell me, I wouldn't
have listened. One invents excuses and arguments and alibis,
and covers one's eyes and ears so as not to see an obstacle to
happiness. Even if I'd known that on campus I was seen as just
a climber and a flunky, I wouldn't for a second have considered
changing my behavior.

In any event, our relationship soon grew beyond the strictly
academic setting, and campus ceased to be the only place we
met. Soon it became normal, for example, for me to meet
Alberto in the Bloody Mary after lunch, or for him to stop
by my place and call up on the intercom to see if I wanted to
get coffee, if I hadn't already stopped by his place. Nighttime
quickly acquired that whiff of deliberate, wanton indulgence
that I had dreamed of in my last years of high school, and
the city then became an enormous palace at our disposal: we
soon fell into the habit of relying on each other to make plans,
though Alberto less urgently on me than I on him, since he had

none of the anxiety my dread of solitude had imprinted on me, or my fear of sinking back into the dullness of days. Soon we acquired the customs of friendship, and the routine and trust of those who have gone through life repeating the same rituals, the same gestures, the same tics; in short, our friendship soon seemed solid and unshakeable, as every friendship does when it hasn't been put to the test and nothing suggests that such a thing could occur.

Images from that period remain etched in my memory, though they're jumbled together, out of order, dislodged from the precise spot they occupied in the chain of events. I don't remember, for example, exactly where to place the image of a middle-aged woman with long blond hair and pencil-thin legs walking over to us between the tables in the campus café, or the image of that same woman standing in front of Alberto and delivering a colossal slap to the face just as he got up from his chair. When did that happen? In second year? Third? It must have been in the spring, because I can clearly see the sunlight shining on the woman's hair as she strode out of the café, and I can also see Alberto in short sleeves, standing up, shrugging, turning to everyone gathered there and saying, unruffled: "She's obviously confused me with someone else—not that anyone could make her listen." Yes, it was in the spring, early June, probably, but of what year? Eighty-three? Eighty-four? Did I go home afterward for lunch with my mother and sister, as I always did during second year? Or did I eat with Alberto and maybe one of his friends in a little restaurant near his house, as we did during our third year at school? Did it happen a few days before that other appalling episode in which Alberto and I found ourselves waiting in line at a phone booth on the Avenida del Diagonal with the barbaric intention, which we didn't openly acknowledge, of calling up the main office of the Law School with a bomb threat just a few hours before an Administrative Law exam we hadn't studied for? And when exactly did we meet Pedro Huarte Vilasoja, the retired professor who ended up becoming a regular on our nights in Plaza Real, and whose suicide

I would learn about years later in the newspaper? When did that young redhead start working at the Bloody Mary, the one we were all in love with, who saved her most private and delectable favors for Alberto alone, as we all knew she would? Can I state with certainty that it was in autumn of '83? And where to place all those faces and bodies and names that passed fleetingly through my life, which I barely glimpsed in the dim light of a bar or the conspiratorial darkness of a bedroom, but can still recall even as I've lost the exact setting where our paths crossed? Yes, I know such questions are ultimately meaningless, especially when the period of time in question, three years, is relatively short, but even so I can't help feeling a certain dismay at my memory's imprecision, as if my inability to place certain details or events in the exact moment they occurred meant I had unforgivably betrayed the past, or even worse, as if an infallible memory would let me reinhabit that past, which, obviously, is pure nonsense.

I do recall, however, the exact moment when Alberto and I started to grow apart, the specific day and time our friendship began, little by little, to dissolve. It was June 7th, 1985, in fourth year, one day before finals. That day, on the stairway up to the library, I learned my friend had decided to drop out.

The reasons that led Alberto to study law differed little from mine. We both shared the same distaste for the subject, the same boredom, and we both managed to pass our courses by studying only a few days before exams. In my case, my aversion to law was bound to yield sooner or later to the regrettable necessity of finding a job and earning a living, but in Alberto's case, since he belonged to an affluent family and at age nineteen had inherited from his grandfather a sum sufficiently generous to keep him from worrying about his future, his dismissive attitude toward school was more than justified by his financial circumstances. This substantial difference between us, which at first I regarded with naive admiration, took on entirely new dimensions for me the day Alberto informed me he had decided to drop out. Until then I hadn't thought of the future as an inescapable demand. On the contrary: the relative ease with which I passed my courses, and the ensuing family tranquility, along with a lifestyle dominated by a euphoric, voracious present, had lulled me into thinking that the future could be endlessly postponed, like that point on the horizon one can approach but never reach. In the cheerful ignorance I had settled into, however, Alberto played a crucial, indispensable role. Sheltered by the safety his character offered me, I drifted into an unreal world on which I, unlike him, had no claim. What made that world unreal wasn't solely a question of finances, or the fact that I, for instance, with little more than a year to go before finishing my degree, hadn't made any plans for my future and acted as though I had nothing to worry about. Rather, it had to do with something broader that was harder to pinpoint: the traits of a fictitious character I had created through my friendship with Alberto, a character who worked fairly well over the course of those years, but one I didn't feel capable of extending outside the context that had given him life. Wearing a hat, smoking a pipe, getting drunk before noon were poses and affectations which, though forced, fit with the world Alberto made possible around him. But they were incompatible with the future that lay in store for me.

Suddenly Alberto's decision revealed all my shortcomings, and a chasm opened up before me that I could cross only by making a drastic, painful change.

We still spent the summer of 1985 together. For the entire month of August, I stayed in the house Alberto's parents owned in the south of France, and afterward, that September back in Barcelona, we still saw each other on a daily basis, drinking deep into the balmy long nights of wine and premature nostalgia. But once classes started up again that final year, everything began to change. My newfound commitment to my future, and my need to alter central features of my identity to meet the pressing challenges of adult life, turned my friendship with Alberto into a temptation too risky to give in to.

Little by little I regained my good study habits, adopted stricter and stricter routines, and reestablished the friendships I had broken off when I met Alberto (self-abasement always finds an easy welcome and inclines people to forgiveness); little by little I began to settle into a lifestyle that inevitably kept me from Alberto and constantly forced me to make excuses that soon became a matter of course. Our encounters grew fewer and farther between, our telephone calls considerably less frequent. When we did see each other, even though we both made an effort to pretend nothing had changed, we hardly knew what to talk about, and before long an enormous, awful distance had opened up between us.

The dismantling of a friendship is a gradual and often imperceptible process, but once it starts nothing can stop it. Unconsciously you lose the habits you shared and replace them with others, and slowly, quietly, the everyday dependence that friendship had implanted begins to wither, and suddenly a day arrives when you no longer miss it, no longer notice how long it's been since you last saw each other, no longer hope, when you hear the phone ring, that your friend is calling; a day comes, or a specific moment, after which the friendship is something inconsequential, a hazy, superfluous memory.

In the end I let go of my friendship with Alberto. There was no space for it in my new life. You can't map out your future looking backward, carrying memories that would only encumber your progress and jeopardize your new plans.

Of course, over the following years I still saw him, but not because he was part of a daily habit, nor because we made a conscious effort to get together, but because we'd bump into each other once in a while on the street or in line at the movies, or in places we had frequented as friends and continued to go to once that friendship had faded, in the company of acquaintances we no longer shared. And while occasionally a glimmer of affection or mirage of closeness would crop up from the past, at no point did I imagine trying to reestablish our friendship; even if we had wanted to, our worlds were by then too different.

Indeed, from what I knew, which wasn't much, Alberto had

changed very little. When he dropped out he told me he'd use the time to write a novel, something he had always wanted to do, though aside from overseeing a few of his family's business deals, I heard he devoted all his time to what's generally called living the life: he went out every night and drank to excess, and on top of that was rumored to have taken up gambling. His lifestyle further distanced him from his old friends: nearly all of them, some more successfully than others, adapted to work routines and settled into an orderly existence largely incompatible with Alberto's habits.

The same thing happened to me. Our paths led in opposite directions, as I expected they would once we began to drift apart. After graduation, and after two years of exhaustive instruction in various courses and seminars that completed my less than robust university training, I joined a modest but promising firm. And even though the excitement of the first year practicing law quickly began to give way to a growing insecurity about my competence in the profession, inertia pushed me further and further into a social status which gave me pride and satisfaction. I now had a fairly wide circle of friends, people who weren't terribly deep or complex and all had some connection to the legal profession. They seemed to hold me in high regard and provided invaluable support for that responsible, levelheaded identity which, over time and with great effort, I had managed to make my own.

This process of maturation, which really began the day Alberto announced his intention to drop out of school, reached its culmination, I felt, when I met Elisenda, a medical student with whom I fell hopelessly in love, and who, just two months after being introduced to me, had already moved in.

At least in appearance, my life was on track. I'd met my own expectations. And nothing suggested my luck would change.

3

NIGHT REFUSED TO fall. Though the sun had long ago sunk behind the tall buildings that stood across from the bar, the sky still shone a clean, electric blue, marred only by an orange cloud drifting shyly across the northeast. The warm breeze rustling the tablecloths and blowing the leaves in the street signaled the end of winter, and some teenagers coming out of a nearby high school walked home in shirtsleeves, their sweaters hanging by their sides. In the patio people came and went, and as soon as a table opened up new customers hurried to grab a seat, before the waitress could clear the glasses, empty the ashtrays, or wipe a wet rag over the plastic tablecloths.

"Spring has sprung," I thought, and the words echoed indifferently inside me, but after a moment there followed a delayed reverberation, textured by a million pulses, and I felt my head filling with chords of feeling, as though everything around me had taken on a musical, melodious quality. Slightly drowsy from the two gin and tonics, in that state in which the senses let down their guard and therefore become responsive to more indirect, subterranean stimuli, I felt a wave of emanations rush over me, emanations from a past remote in memory if not distant in time; images and sounds and scents from other springtimes, other afternoons and other patios, other wasted hours, hours proudly, satisfyingly wasted on the way to a night heavy with promise; fragments of an era long ago sealed, buried, silenced; the slow rhythm of idle days headed nowhere in particular; memories of years perhaps too seldom recalled, or maybe recalled in secret, under the surface, down passageways and fissures in that other life which time had imposed upon me, a life defined by professional success and the obligations of maturity and balance; years and days and evenings which now, after all this time, as I sat in the patio of a bar in early spring, with nothing to do and no promises to keep, emerged again from the tunnel of time.

I called the waitress over and paid for my drinks, along with the coffee Elisenda hadn't touched. I asked if they had a phone. With the pen she was holding and had been tapping between her lips a moment earlier, she pointed to a telephone booth on the other side of the street. I thanked her and began to make my way very slowly toward it.

A rhythmic succession followed my steps; in my head I repeated a familiar telephone number that seemed to mark the beat of a long-forgotten, rediscovered melody: 418-0069. Even phone numbers can become myths, even they can contain within them the key to a complete and powerful world whose minute details are suddenly illuminated when the seven numbers are strung together in the correct order. 418-0069. "There was a time I dialed this number nearly every day," I thought to myself, and then, with slow, affected movements, as though carrying out the formalities of a ritual, I pressed the seven numbers on the keypad. After a few seconds, nervous from the lack of response, I heard the startling rattle of a phone being picked up, and then the sound of a woman's voice.

"You have reached the offices of the Bank of Spain. We are unable to answer your call at the moment. Our business hours are from . . ." I hung up. Clearly, I had made a mistake. Even with the myths of the past one can make a mistake, even in the process of mythologizing one can slip up and put a six where a seven should go, indirectly and unintentionally mythologizing a country's entire economic system, with its collection of coins and stamps. I remembered that in fact there was a seven, not a six, before the nine. 418-0079, 418-0079, 4-1-8-0-0-7-9, I repeated.

I dialed the number again and this time on the second ring I heard the voice of Alberto Cisnerroso. And only then did it occur to me that I hadn't thought of what I would say to him; only then did I realize that a call like this, after so many years of silence, needed at least an excuse, a concrete reason to account for it. I realized I had acted without thinking, no doubt prompted by the effects of the alcohol and the avalanche of memories that a few minutes earlier had overwhelmed me on the patio of the bar, and I thought about hanging up and saving the call for another time, for when I was prepared and knew what I would say and had a justification ready. And then, when I'd already made up my mind to hang up, I said hello; I said hello knowing that after I uttered that first word there would be no going back and no room for second thoughts, just as a person committing suicide clouds his mind and steps into the void, lured by the extreme simplicity of such a definitive gesture. Something similar happened ten years ago, when I called Alberto's house for the first time, not knowing whether our degree of familiarity warranted taking our still-recent friendship to the telephone stage (a qualitative, substantial leap in any relationship), even though he himself had given me his phone number and insisted I call. That time, too, when I heard his voice I was tempted to hang up and leave the call for another day, and that time, too, I surprised myself issuing a clipped, decisive hello, after which there was no turning back.

This policy of taking the plunge, of replacing fearful indecision with robotic and intentionally unconscious action (closing your eyes and surrendering to a physical act that will push you past the point of no return), tends to produce good results. Except in the case of suicide, when drastic actions have, for obvious reasons, far-reaching consequences for one's continued existence, this tactic, when applied to more trivial or everyday tasks, nearly always reveals there was no reason for terror or alarm. The seconds tick by and life goes on, and nothing comes crashing down around us, and when the floodwaters recede and we're finally safe, we breathe a sigh of relief, and even give a patronizing smile as we recall how we were nearly paralyzed with fear and indecision.

My voice sounded gruff and halting, but after a few words Alberto recognized me and responded to my greeting, calling me by name. Once again things turned out to be much easier and more natural than I expected. Once again the world didn't come to an end. I offered no excuses, alibis, or justifications, and

Alberto didn't seem to require any. We exchanged a few pleasant-ries and arranged to meet a half hour later at the Bloody Mary.

The Bloody Mary is an old, roomy tavern in the Zona Alta, in the northwest part of the city. It has an enormous wooden bar at the back of the main room and a mirror that covers the entire wall behind it, holding a vast assortment of bottles on built-in glass shelves. Because of the tavern's generous size, much of the space is hard to put to good use, and the owners' laziness has deprived it of any decoration or upkeep. The tables, a row of seven, sit opposite the bar, by the entrance, against sliding glass windows that look out on the intersection of two dark, not very busy streets.

I pushed on the door and saw that it still stuck. I had to give it a few shoves to open a gap wide enough for my body to squeeze through. I hadn't been there in over two years, but I had no doubt that the bartenders would recognize me, and that I'd have to say hello and go through the rigmarole of catching up. The daily life of bars is made up of an invisible network of rituals that people carry out with astonishing ease, but as soon as one stops to look more closely, one finds in those rituals a difficulty not devoid of merit for anyone capable of performing them successfully. Now, for example, I had to appear happy to see a certain bartender, give him an animated hello, and ask him how he'd been; I needed to be careful not to hold back on the enthusiasm, which would make me look unfriendly, nor overdo it with the joy, which would simply make me look ridiculous. I also had to somehow justify my long absence, which I couldn't suitably do by telling the truth, for example by saying I hadn't gone out in a while and was now a man of seriousness and mod-eration. But neither could I tell a flat-out lie, that I'd been on a long trip, for instance, for this would lead inevitably to new explanations which I wouldn't be able to provide. And no doubt I'd have to come up with gestures and comments and responses

to jokes I'd barely understood, because it's always hard to get a
bartender's jokes the first time around.

Walking toward the bar in the back I felt a terrible weariness,
and I regretted not having arranged to meet Alberto somewhere
else, in the El Paso, for instance, where no one would have recognized me. I was relieved to see, though, that two of the three
bartenders were new, which meant I only had to say hello to one,
a man by the name of Julio. I decided to walk straight up to him
to get the ritual over with as quickly as possible. As I reached the
bar I noticed he had seen me, and I smiled and raised my hand
to wave hello, but then I saw that even though Julio was looking
at me, his face remained expressionless and serious. My hand was
raised, but I hadn't yet waved, so I canceled my brain's initial
orders, and in a display of surprisingly quick reflexes, instead of
waving my hand, I extended a finger in a gesture meant to call
his attention, and ordered a beer. I'll have it at the table, I said,
turning and walking away from the bar.

I won't deny that, despite providing a certain relief, the
bartender's awful memory annoyed me and opened a thin but
unpleasant crack in the pride I took in being a longtime customer. When you've spent hundreds of evenings in a bar and
drunk thousands of beers there, when every corner of the bar
contains stories and memories and boozy confidences, when you
make it a sort of home away from home, a refuge from the world,
when you've learned all the ins and outs of how it works, and
know by heart what it looks like in the different light that shines
in at different times of day, when you've had secrets confided
in you not only by the staff but also by a fair number of the
regulars, and when you in turn let yourself, in a leap of trust, be
seen in irreverent, compromising states . . . in short, when you've
established that kind of relationship with a bar, no matter how
many months or years have gone by since your last visit, you
hope (even if it's inconvenient) that you'll be remembered and
not treated like just another customer.

I sat down at the only table that was still empty, the one
closest to the entrance. Now night really was falling, and the
streetlamps and the lights in display windows were coming on.

Julio arrived right away with the beer and set it on the table without a word. I thanked him and, once he left me alone again, idly watched a couple that seemed to be having a fight at one end of the bar. He held her hands while he spoke, but the girl didn't look him in the face, but kept her eyes on the floor, merely shaking her head. I was surprised to find myself thinking of Elisenda again. It had been less than two hours since I'd seen her, and nevertheless that encounter now seemed like something impossibly distant, like something that belonged to another life or had taken place outside the coordinates of time, in a space without time that was therefore harmless. "Elisenda left me," I repeated over and over, and even though I wanted to find some hint of emotion or gravity in those words, I detected no significance whatsoever. They left me cold. Perhaps if I had known, or simply suspected, that Elisenda was removing her belongings from my house at that very moment, if for an instant I had been able to imagine the now half-empty and deserted apartment that I'd have to return to sooner or later, if I had been able to understand in a flash of lucidity that my life as I knew it had ceased to exist . . . But in the Bloody Mary everything continued as usual, and it doesn't seem possible for our world to be transformed when everything around us remains unperturbed and indifferent. It doesn't seem possible for our world to come crashing down when waiters still come and go with their trays, when a woman orders a *tapa* of anchovies, when we still hear laughter and catch a mixture of scents wafting out from the kitchen, when that man keeps putting coins in the slot machine and the couple we noticed and thought was fighting starts to kiss and coo, when night is falling as it always does, when you're drinking a leisurely beer, waiting for a friend from the past, while you're still part of that small, safe, comprehensible world. No, it's inconceivable (so we deny it) that something could be seriously wrong when all this is happening and everything maintains a semblance of normality, routine, harmlessness. Elisenda had left me, I knew that, but in my mind the fact was only a distant echo. In reality everything remained the same, nothing had changed. Why then should I be alarmed?

I checked the time. Alberto couldn't be much longer. I stopped thinking about Elisenda and began to look out the window.

I wasn't mistaken. A few seconds later, a familiar-looking silhouette emerged from one of the corners of the intersection in front of the Bloody Mary. In the darkness and mist I couldn't identify him with total certainty, but as he drew closer and entered the space illuminated by the bar's outdoor neon sign, I could tell, first by his gait and the elegant, rigid movement of his arms, and then by the brown overcoat that looked like the ones he used to wear when I knew him, that it was none other than Alberto Cisnerroso.

Alberto walked into the bar and bowed, eyes fixed on me. I stood up to meet him.

"Looks like we meet again," he said, shaking my hand.

"Looks like it," I answered, suppressing a nervous grin.

Julio hurried to him, all smiles, taking his overcoat.

"Did you see who it is?" Alberto asked the bartender, gesturing to me with his head. "I suppose you remember this guy."

"Of course I do," answered Julio confidently. "I hope you're not the lawyer who got the guy off who mugged my wife," he said, laughing.

I turned to Alberto for help, completely at a loss. It's not easy to get a bartender's jokes the first time around.

"The other day his wife Susana was mugged," explained Alberto as he sat down and took out a packet of slender cigars from his pocket. "The police managed to catch the guy, but the next day he was back on the street. If Julio had had his way, they'd have sent him straight to the guillotine. Or would you have preferred the gas chamber?"

"No, no, I don't do criminal law," I hastened to clarify.

"Of course, of course, you don't do criminal law," repeated Julio, still chuckling, though somewhat irritated by Alberto's sarcasm.

When the waiter left to hang up his coat on the rack, Alberto looked at me and frowned.

"I trust there's nothing the matter."

"No, what makes you say that?" I asked, surprised by his comment.

"I don't know, since it's been so long since we've seen each other . . . when I got your call I thought maybe something had happened."

I wondered if my friend had said those words with a certain sarcasm, but I saw an expression of sincere concern on his face, which touched me.

"Everything's fine. I had the afternoon off and thought I'd call you. I hope I'm not getting in the way of any plans. Maybe you had something to do and . . ."

Alberto cut me off, raising the hand holding his cigar and waving it in the air to brush aside the smoke gathering between us.

"Don't worry, I still have my evenings free. My schedule is as open as a teenager's. I'm incapable of taking on responsibilities that would give me an excuse to turn down an invitation. Besides, I was happy to hear from you."

Alberto hadn't changed physically, or at least that's how it seemed. Often the image we retain of a person we haven't seen is modified in our memory to adjust for the passage of time. Probably he had changed, just as I had, but in any case I didn't notice the transformations his face must have undergone, because they formed part of a predictable process of aging that I had unconsciously factored, as time passed, into my image of my friend.

Julio came back to ask us what we wanted to drink, and Alberto had him bring us two pints of beer (I had finished the first one) and some olives.

One of the customers sitting hunched over the bar waved timidly at him, and Alberto responded with an austere, almost imperceptible smile. Then he looked at me and shrugged, indicating that he didn't know the guy, or in any case had no recollection of him. A young bartender with Indian features, whom Alberto called Felipe, brought us the olives and beers right away. Alberto spoke a few words to him that I didn't catch, prompting a hearty laugh both in Felipe and in the other two bartenders stationed at the back, whose eyes and ears were on our table. When we were alone again, Alberto exhaled the smoke of his cigar with satisfaction and raised his eyebrows, looking at me expectantly, as though waiting for me to initiate the conversation, even though we both knew that he would be the first to speak.

It's comforting to see that someone hasn't changed. It's reassuring to find a friendship just where we left it, even if in reality nothing's the same and the continuity is only a matter of appearances. It's satisfying and pleasant to drift through our personal history as though floating through a cottony dream, to revisit the sites of our past, places we thought were irretrievably lost, and find every word, every mannerism, every opinion, every detail in its place and intact and ready to be set in motion again, unconditionally and without hesitation, even if we're no longer the same and that world can offer us nothing more than a mirage. It's natural and right to acknowledge the presence of an identity and an era we assumed we had moved beyond, and to restore the ties that once bound us to them when they come back and lay claim to us, even at the risk of slipping into the unreal, or of losing the path marked out by our more recent habits and commitments.

Every one of Alberto's gestures and expressions (a certain look in his eyes, the way he held a cigar, the manner in which he addressed waiters and bartenders, his reiterated use of certain words) found its reflection in memory's mirror, conjuring innumerable feelings and blurring the years during which our friendship had been suspended. Alberto spoke as though we had never stopped seeing each other, as though no time had passed, as though we had spent that very morning in the law school café. And as I listened to him, I experienced a strange euphoria, the euphoria of encountering a way of life that I myself had, of course, at one point judged misguided, but which now struck me as the only true and authentic way to live. Because a long-lost friend is always the bearer of powerful, unanimous truths, the bearer of renewed life aspirations, and in the excitement of seeing our friend again, when everything is exhilarating, we surrender to those truths and aspirations without a second thought, without the second thoughts and doubts and hesitations that come later, once we've again grown accustomed to his presence and realize that ultimately nothing he can give us will redeem us from the weariness and tedium of our life.

We stayed in the Bloody Mary for a little over two hours, time enough to drink three pints of beer each (on top of my first beer and my two previous gin and tonics) and to polish off two orders of olives and one of salted almonds. Afterward Alberto said good-bye to the bartenders (though I, defiant and resentful, didn't even look at Julio when he said goodnight) and we left the bar.

Outside a few drops had started to fall.

"Hold on a moment," said Alberto when he saw that it was raining. He went into the Bloody Mary again and came out a few seconds later with an umbrella that one of the bartenders had lent him. "Let's get a cab, I'm taking you out to dinner," he said, opening the umbrella and raising it over our heads.

We walked in silence toward a more heavily trafficked street where it would be easier to find a free taxi. I looked at my watch inconspicuously. It was eleven fifteen. For a moment I remembered I had to work the next day and it was getting a little late, but it was a fleeting, involuntary thought that I immediately dismissed to turn to new considerations.

An old, familiar force stirred within me and made me feel confident and happy. How long had it been since I had experienced the voluptuous freedom of drifting through the night with no schedules or planned destinations? Had I ever, since my college years, returned to that roving, dilated present where I spent the nights of youth? Maybe once in a while I had experienced something similar with Elisenda, but never as intensely as before. With her there was always a limit, a more or less agreed-upon boundary that couldn't be crossed, a sense of a deadline or a near future watching us from afar and reminding us, reminding me through Elisenda, that the freedom we enjoyed was conditional, on probation, and that my real life, full of goals and responsibilities and tomorrows, awaited inescapably at the end of the night. Now, by contrast, walking alongside Alberto, slightly drunk, any reference to the world beyond the night ahead of us seemed to vanish. And once again I felt that time was on my side, on our side.

"Here comes a cab," said Alberto, stepping from the curb and waving his umbrella in the air.

We sped through wet, half-deserted streets (in cities mobility, too, is a privilege reserved for those who live by night), and we reached a restaurant in just a few minutes, an uncomfortable and overpriced place, but one that serves dinner until the small hours of the evening.

As we suspected, the restaurant was full. "It'll be about a ten-minute wait," the host said. We decided to sit at the bar until a table became free. While Alberto went to order two beers from the bartender and I idly tried to guess which table would open up first and become ours, I saw someone get up from his chair and wave to us from the back of the restaurant. He was a short, stocky man with curly hair. His face didn't ring a bell.

"Do you know that guy?" I asked Alberto.

He looked where I was pointing and clicked his tongue in exasperation while beginning to smile.

"Be right back," he said, walking over to him.

I took over for Alberto and ordered two very cold beers from the bartender. Which is stupid: obviously there was no need to say "very cold." Actually, I cared little whether my beer was cold or lukewarm. But these kinds of pointless specifications make one feel good, make one feel safe and at home. Like asking for just a sip of coffee, a splash of wine, a couple of olives. Just an indulgence, in short. In my defense, I blushed when I heard the words come out of my mouth. The bartender set the two beers on the bar; predictably, they weren't cold.

I saw Alberto, standing by his friend, signal for me to join
them. I grabbed the beers and walked over. Alberto introduced
me. Óscar Music was his name. I shook his hand—a fleshy,
sweaty hand.

"Óscar is dining alone and has invited us to join him at his
table," said Alberto.

"How kind," I muttered as the stocky friend sat down
again.

Alberto looked at me and shrugged. "What else can we
do?" he seemed to say. "What choice do we have?" I seemed to
say back. Having to share Alberto annoyed me. It always had.
Besides, his friend's appearance inspired a profound antipathy
in me.

We sat around a tiny table, our legs bumping underneath.
Óscar Music called the server by clapping his hands, causing
the customers nearby to turn their heads toward our table. At
first I thought that Alberto's friend was really drunk, but after
watching him a for a few minutes I concluded that, regard-
less of what he'd had to drink, he was probably always noisy
and excitable. He was a nervous man, given to booming belly
laughs. He talked almost exclusively to Alberto, but when he
thought he said something funny he turned to me with his
puffy eyes and didn't look away until he had made sure I was
laughing. I felt uncomfortable and downed my beer quickly.
Alberto, on the other hand, seemed to be enjoying himself,
though he kept casting worried glances my way. "What else
can we do?" he seemed to shrug. By the time the waiter
came to take our order, Óscar had already finished his penne
Bolognese. Alberto ordered a scallion tortilla, I ordered one
with potatoes. I wasn't hungry, probably because the combi-
nation of beer and cigarettes was excessive for someone who
hadn't eaten (the olives and almonds hadn't created a sturdy
enough base in my stomach). Besides, it had been a long time
since I'd had so much to drink, and I was beginning to feel
woozy.

They brought us our food (reheated in the microwave, mine
a little overdone for my taste). Alberto asked me what kind of
wine I wanted to drink, but I declined the responsibility with

a gesture of indifference, and he ordered a bottle of Protos.

Every time a woman walked by our table on the way to the restroom, Óscar Music made an off-color comment in a very indiscreet tone of voice. Alberto, while not joining in, would respond with an unconcerned laugh. Paradoxical as it sounds (since Óscar Music wasn't my friend, I had only just met him), I felt responsible for his behavior and turned to other tables in embarrassment, as though apologizing. "Nothing's changed," I thought melancholically, realizing that, at Alberto's side, I was still meek and unconfident.

Óscar got up. Apparently it was his turn to go to the men's room.

"Who is he?" I asked Alberto as our companion limped away.

"You don't know him?" asked Alberto with astonishment. "Music, Óscar Music, you really don't know him?"

He then explained that he was a well-known playwright. The best of the best, he added. I didn't react right away. In fact I was stunned.

"Who would have guessed, right?"

"Not me, that's for sure," I agreed.

"Happens all the time," Alberto explained. "The world is full of guys like him . . . Some bastards have all the luck."

"I'm really out of it. I think I've had too much to drink."

"Best of the best," Alberto repeated, refilling my glass.

The place began to clear out. It must have been past one o'clock. Óscar Music returned from the restroom talking on his mobile. His phone conversation took some precision out of his step, and when he got back he stumbled over one of the table legs and spilled the wine in our glasses. Alberto looked at me and smiled. I was getting dizzier and dizzier.

"I told you, I don't see the point. I don't want to hear another word about it." Then, without a good-bye, he switched off his phone and stuck it in his overcoat pocket. We had finished our meal. No interest in dessert. We wanted to move on to coffee and drinks without further ado. Óscar Music beckoned the waiter. They cleared away our plates and wiped our

table with a rag. Then they brought us coffee and cognac.
Óscar Music asked the waiter to leave the bottle. "We'll find
some use for it," Alberto laughed. We smoked. The conversation, which throughout the meal had gone in fits and starts,
falling back on anecdotes and jokes and mundane observations, found a smoother, steadier course. Alberto and Óscar
talked about literature, not without a certain tone of solemnity.
I hadn't read anything in months. I've never read very much.
I opted to stay on the sidelines, as I had throughout the meal.
Alberto's statements were emphatic and blunt, which seemed
to impress his friend. Every time Alberto finished laying out
an opinion, Óscar turned to me, tapped me on the hand or
on the shoulder and said things in Catalan like "damn, what
a guy." I nodded. We refilled the glasses of cognac several
times. Suddenly I realized that the restaurant was empty. We
were the only ones left, aside from the waitstaff, who hovered
impatiently around our table, not daring to ask us to leave.
Alberto's voice, slow and deep, echoed throughout the room,
and even now Óscar remained silent, listening attentively.
"Nothing has changed," I thought again. No, nothing had
changed very much at all.

When we left the restaurant it was already two fifteen in
the morning. It had stopped raining and stars dotted the clear
sky. The city seemed to float in midair.

Óscar fetched his car from the lot, a red sports car, a
Mercedes or BMW, I think. I squeezed into the back seat,
and Alberto rode up front. We sped off, swerving from side to
side. And then the buildings and plazas and streetlamps began
to fly past the car's miniature back window. I put up a timid
protest. "Never fear, my friend, it's all under control," shouted
Óscar Music in Catalan, at the same time as he searched his
pockets for a pack of cigarettes. Alberto whistled along to the
song playing on the radio and he rifled through the cassettes
in the glove compartment. "You have no music here worthy
of my ears," he said, stopping his whistling.

"Nothing has changed," I thought but didn't say. "And I'll
be the worst off if we get in an accident." Four minutes? Six

minutes? Maybe ten or twelve? Óscar Music turned right, slammed on the brakes, and then performed a quick, violent maneuver that shook me back and forth. He killed the engine. "We're here," he announced.

A long hallway illuminated by blue neon lights and decorated with photographs of Havana opens into a large room with music blasting. Alberto and I are at the bar. Óscar is out on the dance floor. All three of us are drinking gin and tonics. Óscar's don't last long, no doubt because his bizarre, jerky movements make him spill a large portion of each drink. Every time he comes back for another he does a few steps in front of us and tries to get us to join him on the dance floor. Alberto looks at him with a mixture of pity and disdain and delight. I laugh but can't tell whether I actually find him funny. At any rate I laugh. I don't feel dizzy anymore.

"Now you see what success does to a person," says Alberto into my ear while Óscar heads out again, thrusting his hips back and forth. "His new play opens next week," he tells me. Then, for the first time all night, Alberto asks me how my life is going. For the first time the years spent apart return to the surface, the years we barely saw each other, when I didn't exist for him and he didn't exist for me.

"Not bad, hanging in there," I say, raising my voice and shielding it from the blaring music with a hand cupped over my mouth. "What about you? How's everything going?" I ask.

"As you can see, nothing's changed," he answers with a shrug. "Though the years go by," he adds. Óscar Music comes back to where we're standing with two women in tow. He tries to introduce us, but right away he realizes he hasn't asked their names. "Virginia," says one, with a coy smile. "Helena," says the other, not hiding a certain irritation or lack of interest. "This is Alberto," Óscar Music goes on to say, "this man is a genius. They don't make them like that anymore." Then he turns to me: "Virginia, Helena . . ." He looks at me but can't remember my name. I refresh his memory. "Of course, it was on the tip of my tongue. Also a genius," he exclaims, gesturing at me. He offers to buy them a drink, and only the one named Helena accepts, though she does so with the same look of irritation and lack of interest that she displayed when introducing herself. Alberto's talking to Virginia. I move a few yards away, trying to find a place where the noise from the speakers is less deafening. I'm elbow to elbow with Helena, both of us leaning on the bar. "This girl's not very friendly at all," I think. "But it's probably just a strategy, she probably thinks she seems more interesting this way." Óscar Music is dancing in front of us and constantly making strange faces at us, opening and closing his mouth as if he were chewing a piece of meat of colossal proportions. "This guy's hopeless," I tell myself by way of encouragement. I try to think of something clever to say, something to break the ice and surprise her and get her to drop the femme fatale pose. "They should outlaw these kinds of dives," I say at last, satisfied with my comment. The girl looks at me, puzzled, as though she didn't understand what I said. When I lean over toward her ear to repeat it, she grabs her drink and heads for the dance floor. I'm left standing there with my mouth open. Perhaps I wasn't clever enough. Óscar Music follows her. Virginia seems to be having fun with Alberto. I wonder what he's telling her. "No, nothing's changed," I say again. But the boost from the alcohol impels me to action. I turn around and order another vodka and orange from the bartender. Then I ask her for a light. A minute later I ask her for another ice cube. Right after that I ask her what time it is. Finally I go for it and ask her name. The bartender doesn't answer and walks away. Óscar Music comes back blowing smoke in my face.

"Look at Alberto! Look at him!" he says in Catalan, "he's a master. A mas-ter!" I ask what happened to Helena. "Forget about her, that girl's not playing around," he answers. I notice then that one of his cheeks is redder than the other. I prefer not to inquire what happened. Óscar walks over to Alberto and Virginia and begins to dance around them. He crouches down very slowly, rocking his hips; when his rear is about to touch the ground he leaps up and starts over again. Virginia covers her face with her hands and laughs. Then Helena appears with both purses over her shoulder. She grabs Virginia by the hand, gestures emphatically with her head, and drags her friend toward the exit. Before they slip out the door, Virginia turns to Alberto with a look of resignation. "Wish I didn't have to go," her eyes say. Alberto raises his glass in reply. We're all standing by the bar. "What a pair of lesbians," grumbles Óscar Music sadly.

Another bar. This time two men block the entrance. "Three," says Alberto, and one of the men steps to the side to let us in. A dimly lit hallway flanked by raised concrete platforms. A few couples making out. Then a maroon-colored curtain. And then a room that's not very different from the last one. Music and people dancing. A brass rail. Four bartenders behind the bar, three women and one man. More gin and tonics. This time I pay. Alberto talks about a plot against him, in his family, I think, a family plot against him. Óscar interrupts him, out of breath.

Another bar. This time there's a wooden staircase and no bouncers at the door. After that the usual. Óscar knocks over someone's drink.

Another bar. This place is dead, let's get out of here. But first a tequila shot, so they can't say we left without ordering anything.

Another bar. Or maybe not. Maybe it's just the three of us walking up the street, looking for the car. Four or five in the morning. "I'm positive I parked it here, I'm telling you someone stole it." Incoherent words. Alberto recites some lines: "And I asked, I begged for us to not go home again." Óscar repeats his favorite dance: he rocks his hips and slowly crouches down, then leaps back up toward the sky. Things won't stay still. The lights multiply. Finally, a red sports car, Mercedes or BMW, I think. "I'm telling you, someone moved it," Óscar Music insists, annoyed. I have to squeeze in back again. We hit the car parked in front of us. "It's fine, nothing to worry about." "Let's get one more drink," someone proposes, maybe me. Óscar says he knows the perfect place. Five minutes? Ten minutes? Fifteen? A building in the Eixample district. Óscar rings a buzzer. The door opens. Elevator to the sixth floor.

"Where are you taking us?" asks Alberto. A lady of about fifty, wearing a long and very elegant dress, meets us on the landing and asks us to keep our voices down. We walk into the foyer. Red velvet armchairs, candelabra covered in wax, equestrian-themed paintings, gold-footed lamps, multicolored rugs. Óscar speaks to the lady in the corner. Then they serve us cava. A door opens. Out come several young women wearing next to nothing. Óscar has a laughing fit. He claps. "Bravo, bravo," he keeps shouting. Alberto and I are sitting down. The dizziness comes back. Alberto offers me a thin cigar. We smoke. More young women file into the foyer wearing next to nothing. Cava lady of fifty Óscar clapping us smoking. Candelabra velvet corner-door women. I feel dizzy. Very dizzy. Girl of fifty nude candelabra foyer. I close my eyes. When I open them again I see Óscar with his arms around a young woman. They disappear through the corner door. "All paid for, it's all paid for," he repeats in Catalan, still laughing. Alberto gives me a worried glance. "What can we do?" he seems to shrug. "What choice do we have?" I seem to say back. And then I'm walking with a woman named Ivón, holding on to her to stay upright, with a bottle of cava in my free hand. Then a pink room with a round bed, sink, shower, bidet, and toilet in one corner. "There's no need," I try to say. But I collapse on the bed. Hands run up and down my body. Everything's spinning. I close my eyes. I hear Óscar laughing and moaning in a nearby room. Miss Ivón kisses my ear and blows on it. My trousers are removed. Tickling condoms hands caresses. "There's no need," I insist. I open my eyes. Meaningless words. Ivón laughs. I like her smile. We pour the cava. We raise a toast. "Another day, then," she says, stroking my cheek. We share a cigarette. Suddenly I feel a need, an urgent need, to urinate. I excuse myself and stagger off to the toilet. My feet stop in front of the bowl, but my body, like a ship's mast in a windstorm, sways from left to right. Relief. Though not quite—it's not as pleasant or liberating as I imagined. A contained, uncomfortable relief. But relief all the same. I hear the laughter of a young woman named Ivón. I give her a quizzical glance, ready to share in the joke. She's lying on the bed, rolling in laughter. She points at the most intimate parts of my anatomy. Humiliated, I look down where she's gesturing. It has never been rigorously measured, without the veil of self-deception. Maybe its length is minimal, laughable. Though I certainly never thought so. But when I look down at the object of my humiliation I discover with joy that what's causing such hilarity is not this, clearly, but something else, something in truth more embarrassing but in any case less worrisome: I forgot to remove the condom before starting to urinate, and the latex has lengthened and swollen at one end, like a balloon. I breathe easy and also burst out laughing, looking at Ivón, and I tell myself that this girl is very funny and very sweet, and I suddenly feel an enormous desire to embrace her and take her to bed.

In the adjoining room Óscar's laughter echoes like an echo of our own laughter, and in the hallway a voice that no doubt belongs to the lady wearing a very elegant long dress requests, very politely, a little quiet.

4

EVERY AWAKENING REQUIRES an effort of adjustment: we have to recognize the reality unfolding before our newly opened eyes and slowly make it ours once more, shaking off the landscapes inhabited in sleep and emerging from the parentheses that provided a few hours' shelter. But when we awaken after a night of alcohol and excess we find no connection between the world we left behind when we surrendered to sleep and the world that appears before us the next morning, nothing that allows us to reorient ourselves and make the necessary adjustment; we find ourselves in a dark, vertiginous void with no lines of communication to link those two realities, too distinct to belong to a single life, to one sole character. Sleep then appears as the only refuge, as the intermediate space which, though unreal in the strict sense of the word, can continue to lend legitimacy to our existence. Of course, one cannot sleep indefinitely: sometimes a worry crops up on a first rousing, sometimes an external interruption (a ringing telephone or doorbell, a car horn, a neighbor's radio) brings us back to a reality from which we desperately wish to escape. And in these cases we then feel, in addition to the headache and the other familiar physical discomforts, an inner trembling that suffuses every gesture with fear and makes us shiver in the height of summer.

At some point I heard a telephone ring, but either the sound emerged directly from the dream, or I incorporated it into the dream so as not to have to wake up yet. Eventually, though, the insistent sound roused me, and I realized that the phone was indeed ringing outside the confines of my sleep. Even so I couldn't find the strength to sit up and walk to the living room to answer it.

Once I awoke, stray images from the night before began parading through my mind and I writhed under the sheets, trying to get away from them, perhaps trying, as I initially managed to do with the telephone, to dilute them in a protective, harmless dream. Too late. The preceding night now appeared before me as something real and concrete, and little by little, like a large house with separate circuits for each room, lit up in stages as the successive switches were flipped, the different faces and scenes from the night began to reappear in my memory: dinner with Alberto and his friend, the red sports car speeding through the city, the bartender who snubbed me when I asked her name, the sullen Helena who snubbed Óscar, the older woman who met us on the landing of a building in the Eixample, the cava with Ivón . . . And immediately, though slowly, with fearful prudence, I tiptoed further back in time and recalled what had happened a few hours before all that, on the patio of a bar. And again I saw Elisenda seated across from me, and again I heard her words, and even knowing those words were real and concrete, I made them echo inside me with the cottony, ethereal quality of dreams, and I reached out my left arm hoping still to find the warmth of a human body, because while I knew deep down I'd find nothing there but a stretch of empty bed, there's a moment just before we face the inevitable when we believe our will is stronger than all of reality, and until we fill our hands with emptiness and absence, we don't give up on finding, asleep by our side, the person who left us.

I stayed in bed a few minutes longer, curled up in the fetal position, a position a casual observer would perhaps deem forced or overly theatrical, but one I adopted, I swear, with the spontaneity of a reflex action. When I realized I wouldn't be able to find my way back to sleep, I got out of bed and walked around the house, opened every drawer and looked in every closet. Every one of Elisenda's belongings, every one of her dresses, every one of her books, along with the cosmetic products that should have filled the bathroom shelf, and the watercolors she painted two autumns ago, and the photographs, and the dishes her mother gave us that we still hadn't used, and her leather-bound planner that no longer lay next to the telephone, and the compact discs of Brazilian music, and her shoes, and her collection of fashion magazines, and her Mexican trunk . . . all her things now occupied (now that they had physically disappeared) a much more evocative, much more moving space than they had previously been granted. From each one of the gaps left by her departure sprung new sensations, varying subtly and with utmost cruelty according to the object missing. I didn't feel the same standing in front of the bare wall where her photograph used to hang as I did looking at the empty spaces among my compact discs, because in each case the memories they brought to the surface were different. The photograph of Elisenda brought back our trip to the Greek isles, where it had been taken, while the compact discs I could no longer listen to comprised a musical world overflowing with allusions to times spent with her in that apartment. But it wasn't only her belongings that took on, by virtue of her absence, a new and amplified significance; my things, too, acquired an unfamiliar dimension, a sorrowful quality; and while because of their origins those things ought to belong to me more than to her, shared use over time had suffused them with Elisenda's scent and gaze and touch, and now that she was no longer there to give them her scent and touch and gaze, they appeared before me marked by the unmistakable stigma of abandonment, the same stigma that now began to spread across my body. Though the deed to the property still bore my mother's name, that apartment was no longer truly my home, and I was no longer the same. And so, forsaken, confused, trembling in the middle of the empty living room and still in my underwear, I grasped that Elisenda really had left me, and that everything had begun to change.

I could hardly keep from throwing myself on the sofa and sobbing like a child, and I might have done so had the phone not rung again. My trembling ceased for a moment and all my attention narrowed to a single point. I leapt over a stool and ran to the end table where the telephone sat. I took a deep breath before picking up, in an attempt to erase the symptoms of my hurry and nervousness, but also to prolong for one more second the thrilling moment when every outcome is still possible and therefore so is hope. And then I picked up and heard the only voice of all possible voices I could have expected to hear. And in an instant, in a fraction of a second, the voice I hoped for most, the one that could rescue me from despair and solitude, the only one able to end my confusion and bewilderment, was silenced along with every other possibility, by the shrill, pinched voice of Ricardo Maserachs, one of my colleagues from work.

Maserachs's tone was tense and impatient.

"What do you mean what's the matter? You really have the nerve to ask?"

His words took a few seconds to sink in through my disappointment. "It could have been Elisenda," I thought as my colleague spoke. Until the instant I picked up the receiver and heard Maserachs's voice, there was still a chance it could have been her. Everything would have transpired identically: the telephone's ring doesn't vary by caller. Until the last second it could have been Elisenda, but no longer. I picked up the telephone and the voice that reached my ears through the receiver did not belong to her.

"Would you mind telling me where you've been all morning?"

"What's the matter? I don't understand . . ."

But I was beginning to understand. The reality we set aside before surrendering to the inertia of the night does not reappear the next day in a unanimous, harmonious fashion, but rather unveils its various facets chaotically, guided by the fickle hierarchies of memory. At some point during the night I lost track of the immediate future and had unilaterally and unconsciously canceled all my obligations for the following day. And now, through the voice of Ricardo Maserachs, the reality I had shrugged off and ignored reared its head again and glared at me menacingly.

I looked up to the clock on the wall and saw, as I raised my hand to my head, that it was twelve thirty in the afternoon.

"I don't understand," I nevertheless stammered again, trying to stall for time while desperately searching for a convincing excuse.

"Señora Ruscarons . . . the wrongful termination hearing you had at nine thirty-five. You forgot about it, didn't you? I knew it, you forgot."

"Of course not, Maserachs, of course not. How could I forget Señora Ruscarons's hearing?"

Every possible calamity ran through my mind: a close family member had died, a group of armed burglars had broken into my apartment, an ill-placed step had robbed me of consciousness for three hours, my doorman had been murdered and I had to stay at home for police questioning, a pipe burst on the floor below me and drowned the little old lady who lives there, I had salmonella poisoning, a butane tank had exploded . . .

"Elisenda left me," I finally managed to say, in one of those fits of raw sincerity that liars succumb to from time to time.

Ricardo Maserachs remained silent for a few seconds, as though he didn't know what to say, as though the surprise had left him speechless. I then felt a great tenderness for my colleague, and for myself, and once again nearly burst into tears.

"Listen, I don't know if what you just said is true," said Maserachs, abruptly cutting off the feelings that had started to well up inside me, "but at any rate you, as a professional, have responsibilities that you can't just ignore on a whim. You're not a child anymore, you know. Today you had an important hearing, a very important hearing, and you didn't go. You arranged to meet Señora Ruscarons at the office at nine thirty to head over to the CMAC together. She and Luisa spent all morning trying to reach you, but no, the gentleman had romantic troubles and chose to vanish without a trace . . . You probably figured that once again I'd be there to save your ass, right? Well, you were wrong, this time I couldn't, your plan backfired. I had a trial first thing this morning. And Santasusana is in Granollers. So the wrongful termination suit has itself been *wrongfully* terminated. This time you really screwed up. Señora Ruscarons just left. She's gone ballistic. You didn't even have the decency to let us know."

"I couldn't, there was no way . . ." I tried to make excuses, but he cut me right off.

"It seems she's made up her mind to file a complaint with the Bar Association. I tried to talk her out of it," he continued, taking a less aggressive tone, "but the fact is she has plenty of reason to raise a big stink. To say nothing of the lawsuit she can throw at you for damages."

"What did Santasusana say?"

"He's not back from Granollers yet. He should be here any minute."

Maserachs said nothing for a few seconds, waiting for me to speak.

"Oh, for Christ's sake! Give me a break!" he exclaimed at last. Then he hung up.

I paced about the apartment, not knowing what to do, unable to think, still in my underwear, trembling more than before. There exists a degree of helplessness for which an adult's resources are ineffectual and insufficient, a level of vulnerability so intolerable that, falling into it, you regress momentarily to childhood, give up the struggle, and in a state of surrender, await the redeeming caress that will let you breathe again. But the person who could offer me that calm, the person who could transmit, through a maternal caress, enough security for me to face what lay in store, was not only no longer by my side, but was moreover one of the causes of my helplessness. Thoughts and images were interwoven in my mind in a chaotic patchwork without meaning or order. Out of that chaos shot catchphrases like rockets from an island in flames, slang expressions that I grasped at as a last resort and mechanically repeated, unable to string together a coherent sentence: whatever will be will be, one is the loneliest number, time to hunker down, wipe that stupid grin off your face, no pain, no gain—that sort of thing.

I suddenly found myself in the kitchen, dully drinking a cup of cold coffee, the coffee Elisenda made the day before, probably as she gathered her things and packed her bags, probably while I was out getting carelessly, happily drunk. And the image of Elisenda, preparing her departure while I sat serenely with a drink on the same patio where she had just told me our relationship was over, seized my chest with such force that for a few seconds I thought I would suffocate. But right away, before my mind could react, the image of Elisenda disappeared and I saw Señora Ruscarons, gesticulating with conviction from one of the kitchen stools (though the stool now merged with the black leather armchair from the office); and next, or as part of the same image, I saw Santasusana staring at me gravely without saying a word, and behind him, Maserachs smiling cynically and waving a copy of the Civil Code. And then I saw Elisenda again, this time drying her tear-streaked face, and I saw myself in the center of an enormous room searching in vain for an excuse, an alibi, a justification for all my erratic behavior. These and other, similar images paraded through my mind, one by one, pausing only for a moment, just long enough to renew the intensity of my angst, then disappearing to be replaced by others, like riders on a Ferris wheel spinning ceaselessly inside my head.

I rushed to the bedroom for a cigarette. I looked around for a while and finally located the trousers I had worn the night before wadded up under the bed. I breathed a sigh of relief when I discovered in the pocket a crushed pack of Camels with one cigarette left, which I carefully removed and straightened out with impatient fingers. I ran back to the kitchen in search of matches but found only an empty box. I then lit the gas range with the electric igniter and brought my face up to the flame to light the cigarette. I also singed four or five hairs on my head. I straightened back up and drew the smoke greedily into my lungs. More than once, while lighting up in the middle of an embarrassing or painful situation, I had felt that smoking placed me, in a sense, outside of time, safe from the urgency and doom of the present. But never had a drag provided me with such serenity, such company. "It ain't over till it's over," I said aloud as I exhaled the smoke. And I kept smoking, and little by little my thoughts, which for some time had been sluggish, began to flow again.

I had to go to the office. I couldn't stay hidden any longer. Eventually I had to face Señora Ruscarons and Santasusana and everyone else. I took a blister pack of painkillers from one of the kitchen cupboards and washed down two pills with the cold coffee. Then I went back to my room and started to get dressed. I spent more than ten minutes looking for my right shoe. "The sooner I get this over with, the better," I said to myself, and left the house with that strange, intermittent heedlessness that sometimes comes with hangovers and tends to be confused with bravery.

5

IT'S GALLING AND painful to disappoint the cruel, the intransigent, those who watch with an eager eye for us to stumble and fall so they can unleash all the fury of their scorn or their wrath, but it's much sadder and more embarrassing to fall short of the expectations of those who patiently trusted us; it's sadder and more embarrassing and more dire to disappoint those we know will forgive us, sympathize with us, who will undoubtedly offer us their aid and their unconditional support.

I wished, on that rainy, blustery morning, as I walked to work shivering in the cold, that Santasusana, my boss, were not the tolerant, compassionate man that he is, that he weren't one of those old-fashioned men who imbue each and every action with a sort of ethical commitment to all humanity. I wished, on that sad, cold morning, as I bought cigarettes at the gas station to avoid facing the unpredictable look on the face of the clerk at the kiosk, that Santasusana were a coarse and unpleasant man, a man given to insults and tantrums, because then I would have had, if nothing else, the consolation of fending off an attack. Nothing is more disarming than another person's compassion. What can you say to someone who's already forgiven you? What argument can you wield, what face can you wear after letting someone down who placed their unreserved trust in you? How can you take shelter in the pride and theatricality of a fight when you're not even called out on your flaws? How can you not feel the whole burden of guilt when your opponent asks no repentance of you? And how then can you not feel ungrateful, terrible, reprehensible?

Santasusana received me with a look of paternal indulgence, a look free from reproach or sarcasm, a look that was plain and generous. And I couldn't help hanging my head in shame as I offered a halting apology.

"It's certainly an awkward situation," Santasusana began, "because the amount of money at stake for her dismissal was substantial, and since we failed to show up . . . But don't be too hard on yourself. These things happen. I myself have wound up in a similar situation more than once over the course of my career. Unfortunately, the client is Señora Ruscarons, and we all know what Señora Ruscarons is like. Have you spoken to her yet?" he asked, tilting his head and staring puzzled at the floor where I stood.

"Not yet, I was planning to do that now," I replied lamely (I was hoping he'd offer to call her), "after I talked to you."

"All right. So here's what we'll do," he said, rubbing his hands together thoughtfully. "Call her now and apologize, say you ran into some serious trouble and see if you can soften her up a bit, though it won't be easy. Let her say what she wants, and don't lose your temper; remember, the client is always right. Then, this afternoon, once she's calmed down, I'll phone her and feel out the possibility of reaching a settlement." He placed his tortoise-shell glasses on the bridge of his nose and looked at me over the lenses. "Though I imagine by now you know she's threatening to go to the Bar Association."

"Yes, Maserachs said something to that effect."

"Well, don't worry about that now. I doubt she'll do anything in the end. And besides, even if she did . . . so what? Can't attorneys make mistakes? Are we supposed to be perfect? Are attorneys gods? Of course not. Or maybe you're a god and I just haven't noticed yet?" he joked, taking his glasses off again and setting them on his desk.

As best I could, head bowed, avoiding direct eye contact, I thanked him for his understanding and shook his hand. Santasusana seemed taken aback at the gesture; after all, like most people who work together and see each other on a daily basis, he and I never shook hands. Then, as I was about to turn around and leave his office, I thought I saw Santasusana lower his eyes again, as though glancing at my feet.

"Take care now, and don't let this matter get you down," he said, walking me to the door. "And if you think you need a break, don't hesitate to take a few days off. However long you need to clear your head."

Maserachs was waiting for me in the hall, though he pretended to be walking toward the conference room. Luisa, the secretary, a bit farther away, behind her desk, likewise seemed to be in suspense. Maserachs looked up.

"So? How did it go?"

I didn't answer. I pretended not to have heard him. I walked up to Luisa and asked for Señora Ruscarons's file.

"It's on your desk," she informed me.

"Of course, sorry, it's on my desk," I confirmed.

I was surprised to see Luisa craning her neck and discreetly directing her eyes toward the floor, as I saw Santasusana do a few minutes earlier.

"You're not going to tell me what he said?" insisted Maserachs, behind me.

I hesitated for a moment. Maserachs wasn't Santasusana and with him I could console myself by lashing out in self-defense, though my mental state at that moment allowed me only delirious, raving blows.

"What do you think he said?" I snapped back. "Head down and shoulder to the grindstone. All's well that ends well. A bird in the hand is worth two in the bush. Or are we gods? Huh? Tell me, Maserachs, are we gods? Of course we're not. Or maybe you're a god and we just haven't noticed yet?"

I went to my office and shut the door. And I think that's when I first thought about giving up. The mess in my office wasn't the mess that comes from work, it wasn't a mess like the one in Maserachs's office, or Santasusana's office, generated slowly by daily activity, by virtue of consulting books and laws and files and leaving them out so they're handy the next time they're needed; it wasn't a useful or premeditated mess, it wasn't the mess that gives life to a room and is proof of persistent, uninterrupted activity; rather, it was a makeshift mess devoid of life, a mess that neither encouraged work nor showed the traces of a continuous activity, a mess that came from laziness and improvisation, a mess that gave the room the desolate feel of an unfinished construction project, a project abandoned early, in a rush, half-built. As I rummaged through the papers on my desk, I began to talk aloud. "No one can make me subject myself to this kind of humiliation," I exclaimed. "If I don't want to call her I'm not going to call her. And I have no desire to call her. I have no desire to go on with any of this. I'll just let it be and let them come after me if they want . . ." But at last I found the file. I held it in my hands carefully, timidly. On the first page I saw Señora Ruscarons's phone number next to her name, and I knew at once that I would call her. It irked me to admit I wouldn't just give it all up as I had threatened to do a moment earlier, it irked me to acknowledge I wasn't brave enough or cowardly enough to abandon my career and run away. "All right, I'll call her. It's no big deal," I told myself. "These things happen every day in hundreds of offices all over the world. A few words, a little patience, three minutes, four at most, and it will all be over, until the next round."

The conversation with Señora Ruscarons went just as I expected it would. "It's an embarrassment," she repeated, over and over, as I mumbled excuses that only added fuel to her indignation and fury. "You'd better get ready, young man, because you haven't heard the last of me," she fumed. That was the last thing I heard her say before she hung up on me.

I spent the rest of the morning smoking compulsively and spinning around in my swivel chair, once in a while adding a sentence to a wrongful termination suit that was supposed to be ready by that afternoon. It was raining. I didn't leave for lunch. The hours slipped by. I think at some point I fell asleep, but my nerves were in such a sorry state that I had trouble telling the difference between sleep and waking, between nightmares and reality. At five thirty I had an appointment, the appointment originally scheduled for the day before that Elisenda's call had forced me to postpone. Nothing complicated: a consultation about pensions that I took care of in a few minutes. Afterward Ricardo Maserachs came by to ask if I had the lawsuit ready. "Right there," I said, pointing to my desk. He took it and left my office without saying a word. I guessed he was angry with me, and I felt bad for not treating him a little more kindly. I heard him say good-bye to Luisa and then heard the main door shut. It was still raining. I was anxious to hear back from Santasusana. It was seven thirty. He should have called Señora Ruscarons by now. So why hadn't he come to tell me about it? Maybe he couldn't reach her. Or maybe the conversation had gone so badly that he preferred not to worry me. Suddenly there was a knock at my door, and a second later someone opened. It was Luisa.

"I'm off. Have a good weekend," she said shyly.

"Is Santasusana still in his office?" I asked.

"No, Señor Santasusana left around five thirty. He had that meeting with the union today, remember? I don't think he'll be back until Monday."

"Oh, that's right . . . the union. All right, have a good week-end, Luisa."

I would have wandered the streets until I collapsed from exhaustion just to avoid going home, but the weather was dreary: it was raining and I had no umbrella. I hadn't even taken my raincoat. Besides, I still felt confident that Elisenda's decision wasn't final. Though not explicitly, I vaguely hoped I'd find her at home, as I did every Friday after work. I would change clothes and we'd go shopping together for the week. If it wasn't very late, we'd stop at a café for a small bite. Later we'd go to the movies, or go out to dinner, or we'd go to the movies *and* out to dinner, sometimes first a movie and then dinner, other times vice versa, or we'd stay home, watching a movie on TV, and she'd try out a new recipe a colleague had passed along. And we'd sleep together, after making love, or not making love, but we'd sleep together, peacefully, with that peacefulness that comes from knowing that the next day is free from obligations, schedules, or alarm clocks. I'd be at home now if this were a Friday like any other, if it were a Friday from the past, if this were any Friday from the last three years; she'd be at home waiting for me, getting ready to go, perhaps looking out the window to see if I was coming, checking the time on her watch, thinking that if I took much longer the shop on the corner would be closed and we'd have to go back to that behemoth they put up two blocks away where you can't find anything; she'd be waiting for me and would already have figured out what we'd do later: whether we'd go to the movies and/or out to dinner, or whether we'd stay in, whether or not we'd call a friend, whether or not we'd make love before sleeping together peacefully; she would have already made plans and I'd go along with them without complaint, happy to do whatever she wanted that night, because anything's fine with me. But this wasn't just any Friday, it wasn't a Friday from the past, one of so many Fridays from the last three years, it was a Friday from the present, a strange, different present, dreary like the rainy weather that forced me to wrap myself up in my blazer and half-close my eyes to keep out a wet gust of wind. It was a hungover, guilt-ridden Friday, the first Friday without Elisenda, unless a miracle occurred and I came home and found the lights on, and saw her standing in the doorway to the living room with that girlish, flushed smile which, early on, after our first fights, I came to recognize as a smile of reconciliation. I now visualized that smile, picturing the house lit up and imagining that Elisenda had thought better of her decision and come back to me, but immediately I tried to think about something else, out of fear that I'd make the frustration more painful and unbearable if, as was to be expected, none of that happened.

Two hours later I woke up on the living room sofa, legs numb, shirt still wet, with a sharp pain in the back of my eyes. The light from the hallway reflected off the picture frames and outlined my body, curled up for warmth. I lit a cigarette and used the flame from the lighter to check the time: quarter to ten. I hadn't turned on the heating: first laziness had made me put off the task, then sleepiness had made it impossible. From the street came the sound of car horns and roaring engines, making the silence of the apartment seem ominous, unnerving, like the silence of the recently dead, when a sign of life they're no longer able to give is still expected of them. I felt an enormous emptiness in my stomach and remembered I hadn't eaten any-thing all day. I considered going to the refrigerator, where there was certainly something left over from the day before, but the thought of food triggered a dry heave. I leapt up and stuck my head into my bedroom. Through the half-dark I could make out the sheets piled up on my bed, the comforter spilling onto the floor, and my sunken, wrinkled pillow next to Elisenda's, which remained untouched. I closed the door and stood still for a moment, unsure of what to do. I looked at my watch again: three minutes had gone by; it was now nine forty-eight. I walked over to the phone and double-checked the answering machine for any messages (I had already checked when I entered the apartment two hours earlier). I walked toward nowhere in par-ticular and tripped on a shoe on the living room floor. I kicked it with all my fury, outraged at life, as if I were the butt of a joke in poor taste that I couldn't put a stop to. Fine, very funny, now let's go back to the way things were. The shoe came to a stop two or three yards away. I walked over and kicked it even harder. This time it rose a few inches off the floor and landed under a bookshelf. I stubbed out the cigarette in the ashtray, stomped down the hallway, grabbed my raincoat off the coat rack in the entryway and left, slamming the door behind me.

From the cab, as I waited for the driver to give me my change, I saw Alberto inside the Bloody Mary standing in front of the slot machine. "Keep the change," I said, impatient at the driver's slowness.

I hurried the remaining distance to the bar, as if I were late for an appointment or missing something important, as if the seconds I could shave off by quickening my pace were vital.

"Well, look who it is! I didn't expect to see you here," exclaimed Alberto, pressing a button on the machine. "Two days in a row!"

"That's right, it's a two-for-one special."

"I hope you're not looking for an explanation for last night. That was all Óscar's doing. I swear I didn't know where he was taking us. That guy's crazy."

He inserted a coin into the slot and pulled the lever again.

"Well, let's put the past behind us—what's done is done. We've seen worse," I replied, not without a certain irritation at being unable to rid myself of such set phrases. All day I had been spewing them out automatically, and I was beginning to feel enslaved by them.

"You certainly seemed to know what you were doing," joked Alberto, while the voice of a woman with a Galician accent issued from the slot machine: *Nudges: one, two, three.*

"I hardly remember a thing," I admitted.

Alberto raised his hand and held it there, signaling to me to wait a moment. He brought his face up to the screen, crouched down and craned his neck. Then he got back up and looked at the machine thoughtfully. Finally he hit one of the keys three times, after which we heard a few bars of a polka. When the music stopped, three or four coins spat out, which Alberto grabbed as he resumed the conversation.

"I don't remember much either, actually. Do you know how we got home? I hope Óscar didn't drive us, in the state he was in . . ."

"I was wondering the same thing."

Alberto pocketed the coins he'd won on the last pull and took a step back on his left foot as if to walk away, but at the last second, just when it seemed he was going to quit playing, he reached his hand in his pocket and took out a coin.

"Last one, promise. This machine is empty."

"Do you actually think it ever lets you win?" I asked, turning around and walking to the bar, which was right behind us.

Julio saw me from the other end of the counter and walked over, smiling.

"Unbelievable!" shouted Alberto, pounding the slot machine one last time.

He brought over a barstool and sat beside me.

"Evening. How's it going?" said the bartender. "Can I get you a beer?"

Indecisive, I looked to Alberto for a cue.

"I don't know if I should . . ." I said, placing my hand on my belly and gently massaging it. "After last night I think I've had enough. I still haven't completely recovered."

"Nonsense. We'll take two beers, Julio," said Alberto, raising his empty glass. Then, when the bartender had walked away, he turned to me: "A little hair of the dog will do you good. The beer I just ordered will be my fourth, and as you can see, I'm doing fantastic."

We delighted in recalling details and filling gaps from the night before, both of us scandalized by the information the other provided. I had no qualms recounting for him the scene with the condom, and I stoically accepted his teasing.

Suddenly I noticed that Alberto, wiping away his smile, stopped paying attention to the conversation and looked down, just as I had seen Santasusana do, and later Luisa, the secretary. He was staring with curiosity, as if examining a strange specimen wriggling on the barroom floor.

"What's going on down there?" he blurted out in surprise.

Puzzled, I looked down where he was pointing. On my left foot I wore a black loafer, while on my right foot I was sporting a brown ankle boot.

"Latest fashion, huh?" teased Alberto, while I, reflexively, hid my right foot behind its left twin.

"That's not funny," I said very seriously.

I remembered that a short while ago I tripped over a black loafer in my living room, and instead of wondering what the hell it was doing there, I kicked it in fury; and I also remembered that earlier that morning, when getting dressed, I spent a while look-ing for a shoe and thought I'd found it at last; and I remembered, chest now tightening, how a few hours earlier Santasusana had repeatedly cast furtive glances toward the floor where I stood, as I haltingly apologized and awaited his absolution.

Yes, it's sad and dire and embarrassing to disappoint someone who gave us their sincere, unqualified trust, who can forgive us and sympathize with us, who won't fail to help us in spite of our mistakes. But when we turn to them to receive their forgiveness, if we're wearing a different shoe on each foot and our benefactor notices, then in addition to humiliation and sorrow, we feel a monumental embarrassment, a terrible desire to have never set foot in this miserable world.

"Well, to be honest it doesn't look half bad," said Alberto to console me, though as soon as he saw me turn white and swallow the way people do when they're trying to choke back the first signs of a sob, he dropped the joking tone and asked with concern whether I was all right.

"The truth is, the last twenty-four hours haven't exactly been the happiest of my life," I confessed glumly.

I then told him that Elisenda had left me and my career as a lawyer ran a serious risk of hitting the skids.

Alberto listened closely to the story of everything that had happened, first barely suppressing his laughter, and then, seeing how affected I was, with a look of serious, sincere sympathy. And when I had finished my grotesque account he offered a few words of consolation and gestures of encouragement, but I grasped at once that nothing he or anyone else could say would mean much to me. Other people never see the full dimension of our suffering. Someone else's pain can only be envisioned statistically, by way of vague suppositions. Alberto could imagine the pain of a breakup, get a sense of how it hurt to be dumped, comprehend the torment and anguish of someone whose career is in danger. But the details of real suffering are personal and nontransferable. Real suffering, the kind felt by one person and no one else, is always specific and exclusive. It admits no comparisons or rankings or general categories, and can't be recreated in the mind of another. I could tell Alberto that Elisenda had left me, for instance, but I could never describe the images, feelings, and memories that made up my experience of the breakup.

"Anyway," I said, raising my empty glass and ready to move on to a new subject, "we'll postpone our sorrow for one more night. Tomorrow's another day."

"That's the spirit," replied Alberto, raising his glass as well and clinking it against mine. "Reality can kiss my ass."

A few minutes later, during which we didn't exchange a word, a small woman with delicate limbs and features walked over to where we were sitting.

"Alberto, we're going to have dinner at Fernando's," she said coyly, gesturing with her head at a table of six or seven people. "Why don't you come along?"

Seeing that Alberto took his time answering, she gestured again, this time at me.

"Bring your friend, it's no problem."

"Maybe we'll stop by later on," answered Alberto, looking at me with a question in his eyes. "But don't wait for us. We might grab something to eat here."

The girl placed her hand on Alberto's thigh and took a breath as if about to say something, but suddenly, not finding the right words, she withdrew her hand and stood looking at Alberto sadly.

The others came right over. They crowded around us in a circle. Some of them looked at me with a timid smile, which I responded to with a slight nod of my head. At no point did Alberto make any attempt to introduce me. "I told Carlota we might stop by later," he repeated by way of excuse. "Please do," the others responded. There were three men and four women. They had the fashion sense of government employees, and they spoke in bland, clichéd words and phrases. Watching them, one couldn't help thinking of surprise parties or organized group tours to Lanzarote. As they walked out the door, one of the men, the oldest, turned back to us.

"Stop by whenever you want, we're all friends here," he said, adjusting his glasses on the bridge of his nose. "We'll be there late."

When we were alone, Alberto stood up from his barstool and went to the restroom. I got the impression he left so as not to have to explain who those people were. In fact, when they came over to say hello, I had the impression that Alberto felt uncomfortable, as though embarrassed to have friends like those. The night before, he himself had told me that he hardly ever saw friends from college. "Friends are like the skin of a snake, you shed them in time," he once said with a certain sarcasm. And I could tell he wasn't at all pleased to have me think this was his new circle of friends.

While waiting for Alberto, I asked the bartender for the

sandwich menu. I needed to eat something. Each time I took a sip from my glass I felt like the beer was falling into an empty well. I hadn't eaten anything in practically twenty-four hours. When Alberto came back from the restroom, we both ordered sandwiches on soft, English-style bread. I wouldn't have been able to swallow anything heavier. He had Julio bring them to the table that Alberto's friends had just freed up. The remaining tables were occupied, mostly by younger people.

We ate our sandwiches in silence, half-heartedly, chewing each bite with exaggeration. Alberto looked out the window. I thought I saw a new expression on his face, one I was unfamiliar with, although as I looked more closely I recalled having seen that expression the day before, in the restaurant, and also later, on our endless, grotesque nighttime odyssey. But only now did I register it, and only now did it become worthy of my attention. It was a melancholy expression, tinged with despair, which appeared on his face only rarely and fleetingly, as it might on someone relaxing their facial muscles before adopting a forced grin. A burst of laughter from the next table saved him from his distraction, and then he looked at me with a half-smile, wiping any sign of dejection from his face. "Such unpleasant business, having to put something in your stomach to give the alcohol the welcome it deserves, right?" he said, his mouth spreading into a smile.

"Who were those people earlier?" I asked, turning back to my sandwich.

"Who knows," answered Alberto. "Some people from the bar . . . I think I met Carlota first, that short little girl who came to ask if I was going with them. Then she introduced me to the others. Though I couldn't say for sure. It's hard to separate them, you know? They're like a unit, like one huge organism made up of different bodies. When I slept with Carlota, a few weeks back, as I lay in bed I couldn't stop looking around, I was afraid at any moment I'd see the rest of the group right there in the room, panting alongside us. Their latest addition is Fernando, the guy with the beard, the older one. He's adapted wonderfully well to the organism. He's a psychologist. They met him at a talk, a talk

he was giving on childhood intelligence, something like that
. . . Can you imagine? He's just another windbag. They have
meetings at his house. They burn incense, drink tea . . . it's sad."

"Do you see them often?"

"No, not at all . . . I run into them here and that's about it.
Today you saved me from a doozy. The funny thing is, they think
we're friends. Despite the fact that, except for that time I slept
with Carlota, I'm always pretty cold and distant to them. I don't
want to end up one day as the leg or the duodenum. Could you
see me as a duodenum? Could you? Me?"

"Well, now that you mention it . . ."

"That's the risk of spending so much time in bars," he said
sadly. "You get mixed up with all sorts of people."

The noise grew louder as the night progressed. New customers filtered in, groups of young people who found no open tables
and crowded around the bar. The server with Indian features,
shirt soaked with sweat, had more and more trouble pushing
through the crowd. Julio, behind the bar, sang out the newcom-
ers' orders.

We finally finished our sandwiches, and after a good deal
of insistence, got them to bring us coffee with cognac. But we
didn't spend much longer in the Bloody Mary. The young people
around us crowded closer and closer to our table and indirectly
drove us to leave the establishment. We weren't really much older
than most of the customers, but we felt old in their company,
strangers in that bar we had so often considered our own. A tall
guy in a leather jacket bumped into the chair I was sitting on.
He turned to me for a second, but then turned his head back
again and continued chatting with his friends, without excusing
himself. "Let's get out of here," proposed Alberto, standing up.
From the door, through the swarm of bodies, Alberto made a
sign to Julio to put what we'd ordered on his tab. The bartender
nodded and waved us good-bye.

The wet streets led us to other bars, bars I used to go to with

Alberto in an earlier time but hadn't been back to since, bars
that now looked different, too different: some had changed their
decor, others had been completely remodeled. The name of one
bar we headed to stirred a boundless shimmering and trembling
in my memory, but when we reached it at last and walked in the
door, all my hopes were dashed. I felt as though I'd been given
the chance to see the girl I loved as a teenager and, going meet
her with high hopes, found before me a fat, moody old woman.
I could find no trace of the past in those bars, nothing that
evoked the nights spent there. I now felt, as I walked into a bar
with a cold, slick aesthetic, that my memories' physical foundation had been stripped, defamed, smashed: in youth we live as if
everything were going to last, as if certain moments could stretch
eternally onward and the places where they occurred could
remain preserved forever. Alberto had warned me when we left
the Bloody Mary, when I insisted we hit the same bars we used
to go to years back. "Don't get too excited. Going out at night's
not what it used to be. Things have changed a lot," he said. And
he was right: things weren't the same. Nor were the young people
that surrounded us the same ones that packed the bars when I
frequented them. A new generation had replaced ours. Now they
played the starring role. The night had new scents, new shapes,
new sounds. And among them I felt lost and out of place.

I could cancel out, temporarily, the changes that the passage
of time had wrought in me, I could ignore the years I'd spent
exiled from the nightlife of the city, I could forget about my
career, Elisenda, my current life, I could dust off the clothes of
my youth and wander the streets with Alberto as if we hadn't
changed and were still the same people we'd been ten years ago;
but I couldn't stop time from passing around us, from transform-
ing the scene, from ravaging the landscape, from toppling every
single landmark in the city that I hoped to revisit that night.

I studied Alberto. He'd never stopped going to those bars in
the intervening years, and even he looked uncomfortable and
out of place. He drank compulsively, impatiently, and when he
addressed some girl he was trying to flirt with, he was no longer
met with a bashful, promising glance, but with a cold, hostile

glare of rejection that he didn't take politely. I understood better the look of dejection and despair that I'd glimpsed several times on his face since our encounter the day before. I imagined Alberto like a deposed monarch, reduced to begging in lands he used to rule over, a king stripped of his power and now shunned and scorned by the very people who were once his subjects and professed to respect and admire him.

"I can tell, by the color of your eyes, that you've crossed deserts and seas to come find me," he said, rising from his chair to block the way of a blonde woman with a serious weight problem. "Well, here I stand before you. I'm all yours."

"Look, *guapo*," the young woman protested angrily. "I've had it up to here with assholes like you, so let me through."

Alberto held her by the wrist for a moment.

"Pardon me, miss. Perhaps I've mistaken you for someone else," replied my friend with a timid genuflection.

Alberto looked at me and smiled. At that very moment a young man in a plaid blazer with two-day stubble appeared by his side. He seemed to be a friend of the blonde.

"What's the matter, are you deaf?" he asked Alberto defiantly. "Didn't you hear what she said? What's your problem? Think you're funny?" And he punctuated each new question with a shove on Alberto's chest, pushing him harder each time.

Alberto looked him up and down, as though inspecting him. Then he grabbed his drink off the table and offered it to the young man.

"Sorry, all these questions have left me a little dazed. Let's take them slowly. What was the first one? Whether I'm deaf, right? But here, please, have a drink, don't be shy." Alberto turned to me and repeated the question. "He asked if I was deaf, right?"

But I didn't have time to answer. Alberto didn't even see the fist moving toward him, something which I could see, seated in front of them as I was, with Alberto in the foreground and the young man in the plaid blazer a little farther off. I could see the fist sailing through the air, about to land wherever it could: on the nape of Alberto's neck, if he kept smiling at me and asking me about the order of the questions, square on his face if he turned back to address his assailant. I tried to warn him what was about to happen, but it was too late. Besides, he probably expected it. The blow hit Alberto just as he began to turn back around, landing on his right cheek. He fell to the ground, a few inches from my mismatched shoes. His drink flew through the air spraying vodka and orange juice on my head.

I jumped up out of my seat and tried unsuccessfully to stop the young man in the plaid jacket who, not content with the blow he had just delivered to my friend, now leapt on him, grabbed his shirt, and held him against the ground. Alberto looked up at him with feigned incomprehension.

"What's the matter? Wasn't that the first question? The one about me being deaf? Wasn't it? Am I wrong?"

I grabbed one of the young man's arms and pulled, trying to get him off of Alberto, but to no avail. A circle of people crowded around us. The obese blonde implored her friend:

"Let him go, Miguel. He's not worth it."

But Miguel threw all the weight of his hulking body onto Alberto and wrapped his bent arm—the same arm I had tried to pull back but lacked the strength to do so—around Alberto's neck. Even so, Alberto found enough air to keep talking:

"Are you sure I'm wrong? Why don't you check your notes? Was that really not the first question? Then I'll change my answer! Can I change my answer? Is it too late?"

To judge by Miguel's face, which I saw only in flashes, the second blow was imminent. In complete desperation, in a pathetic attempt to stop the fight, I think I might have mentioned the fact that I was a lawyer, although if so no one took the least notice. I thought about grabbing a beer bottle that had fallen on the floor in the heat of the scuffle and using it to hit Miguel on the back of his neck, slick with hair gel, but I didn't feel capable of such a violent action. Fortunately, all of a sudden, when I expected the worst, two brawny bartenders showed up, brushed me off and, with some deft and very professional moves, freed Alberto from Miguel. Miguel offered no resistance, and after standing up, showing that he had calmed down and wasn't going to keep fighting, he adjusted his plaid blazer and disappeared into the crowd, followed by the blonde. Alberto lay on the ground for a bit, looking up at the ceiling, nodding with a slight smile at the two bartenders who were now ordering him to get up and leave. Once he was on his feet, a third employee appeared, grabbed him by the arm and dragged him down the bar to the exit. I grabbed our packs of cigarettes, which, inexplicably, hadn't fallen off the table, and followed them.

Out on the street, I examined Alberto's face under a streetlamp and saw on his right cheek a golden circle with a circumference about the size of a mandarin.

"Does it hurt?"

"What do you mean, does it hurt?" he answered, pulling his face out of the beam of light cast by the streetlamp. "The poor bastard didn't even land a punch!"

It's not nice to get assaulted. It's not nice to see your physical integrity threatened, to feel the weight of a hostile, frenzied body on top of you. It's not nice to realize how vulnerable you are to brute force, or to experience the powerlessness and humiliation that your assailant's physical superiority imposes on you. It's not nice to see how fragile your presence in the world is, how fragile and naive the care and attention you devote to your daily life. It's not nice to find the door of words barred, and to have to submit to a violence you neither want nor are able to wield. And not even the consolation of knowing you're intellectually superior can mitigate the humiliation. It's not nice to have to stand by as an aggressor robs you of your dignity and ridicules your dreams, and for all this to happen outside of reason. It's not nice when the only valid and effective argument is the argument of force, because if you're not the strongest and are certain to lose, then aside from threatening your physical integrity, your aggressor will succeed in shaking the entire edifice of your existence.

I thought about this (though to be precise I should say I *felt* this, since my ruminations at that moment were too abstract to be called thoughts, and generated muddled feelings within me that only later and with more calm I was able to pour through the filter of reflection) while I watched my friend walk a few steps ahead of me, at a rushed, determined clip, waving his arms and making all kinds of signals each time a cab approached, not realizing or not caring that none of the cabs that sped by, brushing against his raincoat, had a green light on. When he saw they wouldn't stop, Alberto followed them with his eyes while shouting all manner of insults. Then, as he cursed the drivers, he saw me lagging behind, downcast and dragging my feet. "If we don't hurry, everything will be closed," he yelled. "Are you sure this is really necessary?" I asked. "It's already really late." "Yes, it's necessary. Extremely necessary," said Alberto curtly. And he kept on walking. And I also started walking again, though at times I felt like my legs would give out, and the only thing I wanted to do was go home and sleep, and forget all about that night.

When we finally found a free cab it was after four in the morning. We got in. Alberto looked at his watch and hesitated a bit, weighing different possibilities. At last, with determination, he said to the driver:

"To Calle Marina. Up the boulevard, that's where I get hard."

The rhyme was juvenile, but I was overcome by a comforting, liberating fit of laughter, as if those words had immunized Alberto (as well as me) to the unpleasant memory of the scuffle. Even the cab driver, for whom that sentence couldn't be anything more than a clumsy, off-color joke, seemed tickled: "Up the boulevard, that's where I get hard," he repeated over and over, laughing as though he had only just now discovered rhymes and found them surprising and magical. He was so grateful he even let us smoke inside his cab.

Heading up Marina, two blocks before the intersection with Diagonal, Alberto told the driver to stop.

"We'll get out here," he said decisively.

There was no bar, no club in sight, only residential buildings and a few shuttered storefronts. Nor was there anyone wandering up the street, aside from an older man walking his dog on the opposite sidewalk.

"Are you going to tell me where we're going?" I asked, intrigued.

"We're getting a nightcap," replied Alberto as he paid the cab driver.

I recalled the place Óscar Music had taken us the night before and was afraid Alberto intended to end this night, too, somewhere similar. Again his words ran through my head: "Up the boulevard, that's where I get hard."

"No, not another whorehouse," I protested.

Alberto tapped the roof of the taxi twice to send the driver off, and then looked at me, puzzled.

"What are you talking about? Who said anything about a whorehouse?" he asked, walking toward a diminutive doorway.

He rang the intercom several times. After a few minutes we heard a sleepy, flustered voice.

"Who is it? Who's there?"

"The hookers," yelled Alberto. "Open up for the hookers."

A timid murmur came from the intercom, followed by a few seconds of silence.

"Alberto?" the voice finally asked.

"No, it's the hookers," he insisted, face contorted in laughter.

"Do you have any idea what time it is?" said the person on the other end, before pressing the button to let us in.

Though by now I had guessed, Alberto told me as we rode the elevator that the voice on the intercom belonged to Fernando, the psychologist from the Bloody Mary who had invited us to his place that night. "We'll be there late," he'd said amiably, though to judge by the heavy voice and halting speech we had just heard, not quite until four thirty, which was the time displayed by an odd heart-shaped clock hanging in the elevator.

Fernando was leaning on the doorframe, waiting for us. He seemed taller than he had at the Bloody Mary, and thinner, too, perhaps because the pajamas stretched around his body were too small. His tiny limbs moved in incoherent jerks, as though guided by orders from different brains. While one hand was raised in a greeting, the other was occupied in stroking his thick, unkempt beard. Seeing me come out of the elevator he repressed a look of surprise.

"So where's the party?" asked Alberto, rubbing his hands together.

"What party? Everyone left hours ago . . . It's almost five in the morning," complained Fernando without much conviction.

Alberto walked into his apartment. I hesitated on the landing.

"Come in, come in," said Fernando, offering me his hand. "Make yourself at home," he added, with forced politeness.

Alberto walked down the hall. We lost sight of him. We only heard his voice:

"Coffee cups, part of a cake, bottles of Montseny mineral water, empty Coke bottles, pineapple juice, a bottle of aspirin . . . Good God, Fernando, what were you guys doing? Where the hell's the booze?"

"There's probably some in the cabinet on the right, under the record player," said Fernando from behind me, as we walked into the room that Alberto was inspecting. But I don't know what you'll find, you know I don't drink."

"As a matter of fact I didn't," replied Alberto. "But it's always good to know."

Fernando offered me a seat and then excused himself saying he was going to put on some shoes. Meanwhile Alberto rummaged around in the cabinet Fernando had pointed him toward. He was taking out bottles and immediately putting them back in their place, rudely, with a scoff. Finally he grabbed an unopened bottle of whisky whose label seemed not to disappoint him too much. Fernando hopped back in the room, tying the laces of his white tennis shoes. He now looked lively and fresh, very different from the sleepy, flustered face we'd met coming out of the elevator.

"Hey, I have to work tomorrow," he said animatedly, with a certain excitement, like a child whose parents let him stay up to the wee hours on special occasions.

"Can I pour you some juice, Fernando?" asked Alberto, taunting, as he placed a highball half-full of whisky in my hand.

I didn't really feel like drinking. I took the glass so as not to irritate Alberto and not to waste Fernando's whisky. The altercation in the bar had quickly sobered me up, and I had no desire to go back for more. I was tired, my eyelids drooped heavily and my movements grew more sluggish and laborious. Nevertheless, even though my body demanded rest and I wanted to sleep, I could still appreciate what a visit at such an ungodly hour meant. I've always been fascinated by how easily things happen in the late hours, how an absence of limits and inhibitions turns the nighttime into an unpredictable terrain and takes you where you least expected. The generous, anarchic nature of the night makes it possible, for example, to wind up drinking whisky at five in the morning in the home of a stranger; its reckless hedonism lets you play a starring role in the unlikeliest of incidents and adventures, incompatible with the daytime life, incidents and events that you, the improbable hero, protected and emboldened by the night, take on naturally and without hesitation, as though the prying light of day would never return. I sat there, in an armchair in a stranger's house, after drifting aimlessly through the night, after seeing my friend get assaulted, after wandering from one end of the city to the other, and now, surrounded by objects that made up the private life of someone I didn't know, I once again felt the thrill of freedom that comes with forgetting the problems or limits or reluctance of daytime existence.

Fernando sat on the floor, knees bent, arms wrapped around his skinny ankles. Alberto, whisky in hand, now examined the vinyl record collection next to the liquor cabinet.

Our host asked where we'd been, and since Alberto didn't answer, I told him briefly which bars we had gone to. Then we talked about our respective occupations. Fernando told me he worked as a psychologist in a school for troubled children.

"Troubled children?" asked Alberto, grabbing a record and turning to face us. "In other words, there are troubled children and there are children who aren't troubled . . . Interesting. Schools for troubled kids and schools for untroubled kids, parents whose kids have trouble and parents whose kids are no trouble at all . . . Really very interesting. Since you're a psychologist, what do you make of me? Was I a troubled child, do you think? At first glance: which column would you put me under?"

"Come on, Alberto, you know what I mean."

"No, really, I don't know what you mean, unless you mean what I mean. What do you mean, then?"

"Let's drop it," suggested Fernando, smiling nervously as he turned toward me. "And how do you like being a lawyer? How long have you been in the practice?"

"Our friend here is a wonderful lawyer," Alberto interrupted before I could answer. "The problem is, sometimes he forgets things. Isn't that right, buddy? Don't you forget things? And you know how important it is for a lawyer to have a good memory. That's why he's considering switching to the fashion world. Look," he said, pointing at my shoes, "isn't that marvelous? Two shoes of a different color. That's what I call original."

I shrugged.

"I can see tonight you're in an especially pleasant mood," ventured Fernando with timid sarcasm.

"Not at all, I can be much more pleasant," responded Alberto, refilling his glass, this time to the brim. "You can't imagine how pleasant I can be. For example I could sing you a lullaby to see if you can get to sleep. Would you like that? I don't mind at all."

"I don't think it's worth it at this point," replied Fernando, looking toward where I was sitting. "At eight thirty I have to be in Plaza Cataluña. We're taking the kids on a field trip."

"We were just leaving, weren't we, Alberto?" I proposed, setting my glass on the coffee table.

"Isn't that adorable? Rather than sleeping in on a Saturday morning, he's taking his troubled kids on a field trip. And here we are ruining his night! Of course it was you who invited us here . . ."

"I'm not complaining," Fernando countered patiently. "I already said I'm probably not going back to sleep, so I don't mind if you stay a little longer."

"Right, right, the benevolent psychologist forgives us," said Alberto, throwing a record on top of the plastic cover of the turntable and sitting down on the sofa. "You know what? Everything would be a lot simpler in this world if there weren't so many good people like you."

"Come on, Alberto, drop it already," I interrupted. "It's really late, and we should be going."

Alberto stared at me for a few seconds, first with a look of fury, then with a contemptuous smile, and continued.

"No, really. Life would be much simpler if you were all as nasty as I am. The only thing people like you do is complicate matters. Why do you insist on saving the world? Let it be and don't make such a fuss."

"What do you mean?" I burst out. "Who said anything about saving the world? You don't know what you're talking about. We really have to go."

"Leave if you want. I'm staying here with my friend Fernando. You heard what he said, he doesn't mind if we stay a little longer. Right, Fernando? Isn't that what you said?"

Fernando didn't answer, he just reached out and took a chocolate cookie from the table.

"Look at him!" he shouted, pointing at Fernando. "Look at how comfortably he's settled into his selfless, compassionate forties. Today he'll play ball with his troubled children. He's happy. And he feels sorry for me. 'Poor Alberto, he's lost his way, he doesn't like anything, he hates people,' he's thinking now, listening to me talk and nibbling his cookie like a bird. Well you're wrong, friend, I don't hate people any more than you do. It's just that I don't hold myself in such high regard. But don't fool yourself, no matter how much ball you play with your kids, you're not better than me. Do you really think you're helping them? Do you really think you're doing them any good? Messing with them, that's what you're doing. We all come into this world with our share of suffering: some get a lot, some get a little, but not even Mother Teresa can keep people from getting their share. Of course, good people like yourself make the whole process that much more painful and disgusting. That's what your kindness gets you: you toy with people's suffering, you pervert it, you haggle over it, and all so you can sit there now with your ridiculous, smug, liberal tennis shoes and look at me with pathetic condescension. Save yourself instead, the rest of us will get along fine without you."

"What's gotten into you, Alberto?" I snapped. "You've had too much to drink, and now you're talking nonsense."

Then Alberto refilled his glass and turned to me with blood-shot eyes.

"There's no such thing as too much, my friend, there's no

such thing. Of course, when you're successful, you acquire a special sense of moderation, isn't that so? Sure, a respectable lawyer has to maintain a certain balance at all times. You have to behave, right? But tell me, why the hell do you have to? And what if I have no desire to behave, what if I want to drink like a fish and say whatever I please? Tell me, what then? Do you find the scene unpleasant?"

"Actually, yes, I do find it pretty unpleasant," I shot back.

"Come on, let's change the subject," Fernando pleaded.

"Change the subject? Change the subject?" repeated Alberto in shock. "I thought there was only one subject, just one: your stupidity. And now *he* comes along and tells me I'm ridiculous. And the poor guy has turned into a run-of-the-mill lawyer . . . He always said he hated the law and would do anything but practice. How easy it is to sell out! What's the matter? Do you feel special with your absurd outfits and your cheap ties? Do you enjoy administering justice to people you don't even know? Or do you do it only for the money?"

"Not all of us were lucky enough to be born millionaires," I said without thinking. "We can't all spend our lives bumming around and squandering the family fortune."

"Well, well. It was bound to come out," said Alberto, clapping. Sooner or later it was bound to come out. The typical excuse. An age-old excuse which throughout history has let vulgar idiots like you justify their own degradation. I didn't expect you to sink so low, to have such limited intelligence. Are you suggesting you became a lawyer out of necessity? Come on, who are you kidding? You became a lawyer for the same reason that this guy takes care of troubled kids: to be someone in the eyes of others, to escape your own vulgarity and pathetically sigh with satisfaction at the end of the day. Bumming around! I remember a time when you didn't mind bumming around so much. But of course, now you're supposed to have matured, right? In the end you're all the same. Satisfying your petty bourgeois narcissism: that's what your lives amount to. And what's worse is that you can't stand to see someone who doesn't put up with that crap. Bumming? What do *you* know about bumming around?"

Alberto stopped talking and looked at me, waiting for a response, but I chose to say nothing. I pretended to read a brochure about Finland I found in the folds of the armchair I was sitting in.

Alberto made a dismissive gesture with his hand, like shooing a fly. The gesture meant, "Yes, let's drop it, you wouldn't say anything worthwhile anyway."

Fernando seized those few seconds of silence to get up and walk over to the record player. "We could all do with a little Charlie Parker," he said in a conciliatory tone.

"Well, isn't he a sappy bastard," murmured Alberto, settling into the sofa.

Fernando placed the needle on the turntable and returned to his seat.

The music immediately took over the room and propped up our silence. I opted to remain silent until Alberto regained some calm. Now, even at a low volume, the music poured out of the speakers and seemed to neutralize the tension. Alberto, who wouldn't stop moving around in his seat while we were arguing, now leaned back and tilted his head away from where Fernando and I were sitting. The lack of movement made me think he had fallen asleep, but I dismissed that possibility when I saw his right hand, which hung over the armrest, still holding his glass of whisky. "If he had fallen asleep, the glass would have slipped from his hand," I reasoned. And I was wrong. Fernando, who no doubt had reached similar conclusions, and was understandably concerned about the carpet beneath Alberto's whisky, crept over to him and, making a few sounds that Alberto didn't respond to, carefully removed the glass from his hand.

"He's out cold," he said, setting the glass on the table and sitting back down on the floor, but this time next to my armchair, like a cat curled up at my feet.

"I'm sorry," I apologized, "We shouldn't have come."

"Don't worry, these things happen. Besides, it's not your fault." Fernando cast a quick glance at Alberto and, lowering his voice, went on. "You never know with Alberto. He can be the sweetest, most attentive man in the world, or, if you get him on a bad day, the cruelest and most selfish. Today we had bad luck. In any case, it's not the first time he's made a scene like this."

"I thought you two barely knew each other," I said, intrigued.

"We haven't known each other for long, it's true—four or five months, I think, but in that time we've seen a lot of each other. And I'm starting to figure out what he's like, you know?" He signaled to me with his chin. "What about you? How do you know him?"

"We were good friends at university. But I haven't seen him in years."

"You think he's changed?" asked Fernando, not stressing the interrogative tone, as if he guessed at the answer.

"Well, at first I didn't think so, I thought he hadn't changed much . . . But now I don't know. I've never seen him like tonight," I said. "I think . . ."

But suddenly I stopped, for I had the unpleasant feeling that I was betraying my friend by talking about him with someone I hardly knew.

"To tell you the truth, I worry about him," Fernando went on, picking up the conversation. "I've grown fond of him, and I don't like to see how he's ruining his life. He resents everyone, but first and foremost himself. *Il n'est pas bien dans sa peau*," he said in near-perfect French. "And you can't live like that, you know? He should do something, he should face up to the fact that he can't keep going down this path. Someone should help him before it's too late. And I can't—he looks down on me, as you just saw. He doesn't take me seriously . . . Though I know in his way he likes me."

"And how do you want to help him?" I asked.

"I don't know, maybe by making him see that he has to grow up, he can't keep behaving like he's twenty years old. He's stuck at an age he should have outgrown, and he can't stand the fact that others don't act like him. He doesn't understand why other people change, do things, plan their future, figure out their lives. He sees all that as a betrayal, and that's why he's so angry at everyone. Having money has ruined his life. He doesn't do anything, and no one finds their place in the world unless they do something. It's sad. Alberto is smarter and more capable than anyone I know, he could have done whatever he set his mind to, but nothing interests him. He gives up on everything, he closes every door. And how old is he now? Thirty-three? Thirty-four?"

"In theory he writes. Or at least that's what I thought."

"You said it: in theory. That's what he says, that he writes. But when does he write, if he spends most of his time drunk? It's just an alibi, an excuse to continue doing nothing, to not face his own life. If he likes writing, he should write, but he should take it seriously. Books don't write themselves, you know. Being smart and witty isn't enough. It takes work, effort, discipline, passion . . . And our good friend here wants nothing to do with those things. On the contrary: he looks down on perseverance, enthusiasm, personal effort. He thinks it's all cheap and degrading, that it's beneath the dignity of a superior being like himself. But what the hell does he think life is? A series of brains strutting down the catwalk of intelligence? Does he think it's enough to go bar-hopping, squandering his intelligence and wit trying to seduce a different woman every night? Ultimately he knows he can't go on like this . . . Would you like a cookie?"

I declined his offer and lit a cigarette, studying Alberto, asleep on the sofa: his left hand propping up his forehead in a meditative pose, his right hand, now empty, bent slightly toward the floor, his legs folded into a perfect triangle. Even when he surrendered to a state of rest he maintained his elegance. Not even the bar fight had managed to wrinkle his silk shirt or corduroy pants. His hair looked as though it had just been combed, as though it were ten thirty at night and he had just left his house. And when I saw him like that I felt that Fernando's observations, as correct as they had just sounded, seemed ridiculous and melted away before that perfect image of self-assurance and nobility.

Fernando, following my eyes, turned to look at him, too. After a few minutes, placing his chin on his knuckles, Fernando leaned slightly forward and craned his neck, as if trying to make sense of something.

"Hey, what's that on his cheek?" he asked, intrigued. "Did he get hit?"

I hesitated a moment before answering. Finally I said:

"The taxi slammed on the brakes. He hit his head against the front seat. But don't worry, it's nothing serious."

When we stepped outside, day was starting to break. A fickle, vertical light cast a yellow glow onto some buildings and left others cloaked in night shadows. In the street, delivery trucks and the occasional vehicle of someone on the early shift mixed with the faster, louder cars returning from a night out, and likewise on the sidewalks, as we walked toward the parking garage in search of Fernando's Renault 5, we saw people heading home after a rough night (as Alberto would have said) alongside others getting ready to start a new day of work: a beefy young man, wearing a blue smock and carrying a huge basket of tomatoes and onions, walked past a bench where a young couple, perhaps caught off guard by the fast-approaching morning, suddenly gripped each other and entwined their tongues in an exaggerated rush; a little further on, a group of five or six teenagers, belting out an off-key rendition of their soccer team's anthem and clapping incessantly, forced a middle-aged woman with Asian features, dressed in a muted, frayed tulle, to alter her route and take refuge in the entrance to a greengrocer's, which an employee, pencil between his teeth, was just about to open.

The city emerged in confusion, and neither of the two contrary, conflicting realities that mingled in its streets at that wavering hour seemed believable. I walked slowly alongside Fernando, while Alberto recited endless poems and had to stop every few steps to remember a forgotten line, clutching one last bottle of whisky that neither Fernando nor I had been able to wrestle away from him. And I suddenly felt all the sadness of that incomprehensible crossing, all the strangeness of those two contradictory worlds, neither of which, I told myself, could give me shelter or rest. As we passed by a bakery, I caught a whiff of fresh-baked croissants through the shutters, and that aroma, which at any other time I wouldn't have noticed, awakened in me an intense yearning for ordered family life, for a secure, comforting life full of protection and care. And perhaps because the fatigue had weakened my body's control mechanisms, I couldn't keep two tears, big as cherries, from welling up in my eyes, blurring my vision and forcing me to fake a lengthy yawn so my companions wouldn't notice I was crying.

We walked three or four blocks and finally reached the garage. Fernando had insisted on giving us a ride home. "I won't take no for an answer," he said, silencing my protestations and putting on a suede jacket over his pajamas. "I'll drop you off, come back here, take a quick shower, and be good as new, ready to start the day."

Given that I lived on Plaza Molina and Alberto up in La Bonanova, it would have made sense to drop me off first and continue north on Balmes. But Fernando, seeing the state Alberto was in, must not have wanted to be stuck alone with him. Without explanation he chose an alternate route instead of taking the most logical one, and in so doing avoided dropping me off first.

The Cisnerroso house, located on a narrow little street parallel to the Paseo de la Bonanova, was a free-standing three-story building built in the middle of the nineteenth century. A few yards away, separated from the main building by a row of cypresses, Alberto's parents had built a small, two-bedroom house, with its own bathroom and phone line. Originally the building was for guests, but it eventually became Alberto's home, despite certain objections from his brother Santiago. By the time I met him at university, he had been living there for two years.

Fernando pulled up in front of the gate. Alberto lay in the back seat, tracing with his finger the curves of a crack that ran diagonally across the lining of the car ceiling.

"Here we are," I told him.

Alberto registered my words with a slight smile that gave his face a look of kind repose. He studied me for a moment and then grabbed the two front seats to pull himself up. Judging by the trouble he had finding the door handle, I figured he'd need help getting to his house.

"Do you have your keys? Do you want me to help you to the door?" I asked as he climbed out of the car.

"Relax, I got it," he said just before tripping on the curb and nearly crashing onto the sidewalk, a fate he avoided by grabbing hold of a providential lamppost.

I got out of the car, closed both doors and stuck my head in through the passenger-side window. "I'll be right back," I told Fernando.

"Yeah, you'd better go with him," he answered. Then he turned back toward Alberto, who was still hanging on to the lamppost. "Take it easy, Alberto. See you later."

We stumbled the short way to the gate. After several failed attempts on Alberto's part, I eventually managed to stick the right key into the lock on the metal gate. Once we were inside the yard, which had hardly changed since when I used to come visit the Cisnerrososes on a regular basis, Alberto made a course for the dog house, next to one corner of the wrought-iron fence. The dog was asleep. When it heard our steps it raised its head a moment and, seeing its master, lay down on its paws and went back to sleep. Alberto bent down and patted its muzzle. Then we continued through the yard. On two occasions I had to hold Alberto up by the forearm to keep him from falling. We crept around the main house, signaling to each other to keep quiet, and reached the back yard, where Alberto's guest house stood.

"I'd invite you in, but Fernando's waiting, and I think he's had enough for one night," said Alberto, leaning on the door.

"Yeah, I'd better go," I answered. "I'll call you tomorrow."

As I started to walk back through the yard I heard Alberto call me. I turned around.

"Hey, that night we just had, I'd like it stricken from the record," he said. "Don't hold it against me."

"Don't worry," I smiled.

Fernando was listening to the news while waiting. When I got into the car he turned off the radio. He probably intended to talk more about Alberto, but I was too tired and struggling to keep my eyes open, without success. The whole way home we didn't exchange more than two or three perfunctory words.

When we got to my place, I thanked him for his generosity and said good-bye.

A vigorous spring sun cast its rays onto the front door to my building, and in the windowpanes, as I searched for my keys in the folds of my pockets, I caught sight of my own haggard face.

6

TOO QUICKLY WE grow accustomed to the charms of the one we love. Too quickly the qualities we valued so highly are diluted by the daily habits of a shared life, and we stop paying attention to them. And we discover that what made us fall in love didn't bring in its wake, as we first thought it would, a hidden, mysterious world. Because we fall in love less with a gesture performed with exquisite precision, or the unsurpassed beauty of a face, than with what that gesture or that face seem to conceal. Trusting in that promise, our imagination takes wing.

Every one of Elisenda's features, every gesture, every glance, every word were for me, at first, only the outer manifestation, precise and exquisite, of a boundless, magical world, like the cherry you taste before cutting into the cake. Elisenda's smile, her blond hair, and the green color of her eyes were not my end goal; they weren't, so to speak, an end in themselves. Rather, they were the doorway to a mysterious, redemptive region, free from the dull, wretched yoke of everyday life. When she was introduced to me, at a dinner put on by mutual friends, and I saw her for the first time and gazed at the radiance of her face and the soft, round contours of her figure, my body responded sexually—maybe her smile as she offered me her hand gave me an erection—but at the same time, perhaps as part of the physical response, through her radiant face, her perfect figure, her gentle smile, I thought I'd seen something wholly unprecedented, something (and I can only call it "something," since nothing about it matched any concept then known to me) which seemed to be the repository of every answer, seemed to contain within it the keys to my very existence, something which, in short, once unstopped would set free all the happiness that I could lay claim to in this life.

Predictably, after that first encounter, I succumbed to an imperious need to win Elisenda over, to make her mine. Yet the desire for possession wasn't directed at her body, or her smile, or her intelligence, all of which were only secondary goals; what I hoped to possess, what I wanted to gain and make mine forever, were the depths that her body and her smile and her intelligence hinted at. I didn't realize (no one in love does) that she could never open the doors for me to those redeeming depths, and she couldn't do so simply because that desired world existed solely in my imagination, and I had created it out of my own history, my hardships, my traumas, my hopes, my sorrows. In truth, what I hoped to gain was inside me more than inside her.

When I got her to come live with me I was happy, happy like a child about to open a present, happy like a town on the eve of a festival, happy like the runner who rounds a bend and catches sight of the finish line. I had the cherry between my lips. The cake remained. During the first weeks, maybe during the first months (it's hard to chart passion on the coordinates of time), I watched in amazement as my life organized itself around a thrilling, all-consuming current that erased each of my worries, that cleared away all my troubles, that wiped from the map anything that didn't have a direct connection to Elisenda. But the days of that overpowering, ordering force were numbered, because it fed on expectations that were doomed to failure from the outset.

Love is a promise that is never wholly kept. Strangely, though, its failure hardly hurts at all. There's no precise moment, for instance, when we confront disappointment, no precise moment when the illusions are shattered. We give up on love and barely realize it, like someone who grows tired of waiting for a letter and eventually forgets to check the mailbox each morning. Gradually the body falters, the nerves grow numb, the intensity of sensation dwindles. And faced with a lack of signs that would prove its existence, we start to forget about that hidden world we had glimpsed in the eyes of our beloved. We searched for it, spurred on by its apparent proximity, and for a time the search provided us with a mirage of happiness. Slowly, imperceptibly, the predictable, everyday world we thought we had finally escaped pulls back the veil drawn over it by love, and imposes its heavy law.

And even though we still have the cherries, even though
we can still enjoy the charms of the person we live with, once
the sublime halo we granted them vanishes, and the mysterious breath which gave them life disappears, we eventually grow
numb.

Did I stop loving Elisenda then? Good question, very good
question.

Even as my expectations were shattered, even as the idealized
Elisenda lost her aura, our relationship formed new ties which,
while of a very different nature from the ones that had bound us
together at first, grew sturdier and more stable with each passing
day. Admiration, tenderness, the pleasure of finding affinities and
shared tastes, the pride and satisfaction of knowing that someone
is waiting for you, the reliable comfort of affection, had silently
taken the reins of the relationship. While at first my dependence on Elisenda had sunk its roots into an anarchic, troubled
terrain where I stumbled about, blindfolded, now, by contrast,
that dependence followed much more routine, logical rules. Yes,
I loved her, I still loved her, but now my love was of this world.
It no longer responded to a magical, impossible impulse, but
rather to a pragmatic, everyday organization in which love, like
work or existential angst, had a set place and specific, clearly
designated functions.

Caught in the trap of reality, my love became calmer, more
functional, more ordinary, and this made me experience my relationship with Elisenda as something invulnerable and inseparable
from my future. She was a part of my life just as my physical
attributes were, or my habit of drinking a glass of water every
morning right after waking up. Far behind me lay the time when
I saw threats on all sides, when a glance at a stranger, or a minor
spat, would put me on the lookout and fill me with apprehen-
sion. Elisenda had become a part of me just as I had become a
part of her. And no one fears that a part of them will suddenly
break off. For me it was inconceivable that my relationship with
Elisenda could end, that our lives could separate and exist independently of one another.

That's why the afternoon when Elisenda told me in the patio

of the bar that our relationship was over I gave no credence to her words. It didn't seem possible that her decision could be carried out. If someone suddenly stopped me on the street to tell me I was missing an arm or a leg, I wouldn't have believed them any more. It was impossible, it was unthinkable, it was unbearable . . . and nevertheless it had happened.

When I awoke at three in the afternoon on Saturday, the first thing I remembered was that seven hours earlier, when I got home, I listened to a message from Santasusana on the answering machine. I got out of bed and, after drinking not one but three glasses of water, walked back to the living room and listened to the message again.

"Hi, Santasusana here. It's ten thirty on Friday night. I see you're not in. I meant to call earlier but wasn't able to." Here a three- or four-second pause followed. "So . . . look, I spoke to Señora Ruscarons this afternoon." Another pause. "I'm not going to lie, she's very upset. And I wasn't able to calm her down, although eventually I think she'll come around and we'll reach a settlement . . . Anyway, I just wanted to let you know how things went, but we'll talk later. I have to leave and don't know when I'll be back, but you can call me tomorrow after five, or anytime on Sunday. Otherwise, see you Monday at the office. Have a good weekend."

I listened a second time. I showered, got dressed. I ordered a pizza by phone, and it arrived in twenty minutes. I ate it in front of the television, watching a children's movie. The pizza delivery guy had a nose ring. As I ate the pizza and watched a dog save the life of a boy about to drown in a river, I thought about the delivery guy and told myself that with a nose ring your troubles must be less trouble. Having a piercing in your navel, or lip, or eyebrow, or glans—a Prince Albert, I think they call it—must raise you above whatever circumstances you're subject to. You can be fired from your job, you can lose your girlfriend, you can suddenly discover that the front wheel of your moped is speeding over the wet asphalt toward that lamppost up ahead, you can even find out that you've got some kind of incurable cancer and have two weeks to live, but you've still got the nose ring attached to you, and for as long as you can hold on to it you'll still feel special, you'll still have that identifying mark, an artificial sign that constantly declares, "Here I am." Even if you die, even if your head is bashed in by the lamppost and you're sprawled out lifeless on the street, even if cancer robs you of your life in a hospital bed, you'll still have the nose ring; you'll still be the guy with the nose ring to the passerby who runs over in shock to the scene of the accident, you'll still be the guy with the nose ring for the nurse who comes to the hospital room alerted by the sobs of a family member—"we lost the guy with the nose ring," she'll tell her coworkers. Life is full of unpleasant surprises, of accidents, humiliations, and dangers, but a nose ring makes everything much more bearable, because whatever happens, an outward symbol still identifies you, still reminds you of who you are. And as I thought about all this and ate the pizza, the image of the delivery guy's nostril appeared before me, a punctured, cavernous nostril, and I lost my appetite and had to set aside the half-eaten pizza, and I thought to myself that I could never get my nose pierced, nor my navel, nor my eyebrow, much less the tip of my penis.

I looked at my watch. It was four twenty. I couldn't call Santasusana back yet. Besides, I wasn't sure I wanted to. His message was pretty clear: things looked bleak. Señora Ruscarons would file a complaint with the Bar Association (if she hadn't already) and I'd be up a creek, as Maserachs said. But how far up? Would I have to give my client financial compensation? I had no idea what the consequences could be for my blunder. In the Legal Practice courses, in Professional Ethics class, we had studied the various infractions a lawyer could commit, along with their corresponding sanctions. But that was over seven years ago. I didn't remember a thing, and I didn't feel up to digging through the notes I kept stored away (but not organized) in some closet at home. Just as I started repeating sayings and catchphrases the day before, now legal terms came to mind. Some of them I even recited aloud: "six years and one day," "maximum penalty of six months in jail and a fine of 600,000 pesetas," "sentenced to prison," "the accused is guilty of a crime against the state." Soon I couldn't help laughing, but then I once again felt lost, forsaken, utterly alone. I thought of Elisenda, missed her, needed her as I had never needed her before. I saw her face throughout the house. I heard her voice. But then the voice suddenly changed and I heard another: "We find the defendant guilty." Or perhaps it was still Elisenda's voice, filing separate charges. I paced around the room, seized by a panic attack. The worst thing about having multiple troubles is that you never know which one you're dealing with at a given time. Or perhaps you deal with all of them at once, but in that case you can't tell them apart, you can't establish boundaries between them, and it's as though you're not suffering from anything specific, as though you've given yourself over to suffering in a pure state, with no reason or cause or point of reference in the real world. My heart pounded in my chest and my palms began to sweat. Who said I had to suffer like that? All I had to do was get my nose pierced and start delivering pizzas!

I picked up the phone and dialed the number for Elisenda's parents. She didn't say she was going to stay with them, and I hadn't even thought to ask her where she planned to go. But that made the most sense. Before she moved in with me she lived with her parents. She got along well with her parents. She spoke every day with her parents, especially her mother, whom she loved very much. It made sense for her to go there. Girls from a good family, and Elisenda was one, go home to their parents' house when they have problems with their husbands. Unless . . . unless there's another man. *Another man.* For the first time I considered that possibility. I hadn't thought there could be *another man* before. There couldn't be. Not for Elisenda. The phone at the Riuses' house began to ring. Two rings, three rings. "What can't be, can't be—until it is," my grandmother used to say. Four rings. The phone started to slip out of my sweaty hand. What if this was one of those times when, even though something couldn't be, it was? Someone picked up on the other end of the line. "Hello?" It was the voice of Señor Rius, retired insurance agent, lover of golf and of Catalonia. "Hello?" repeated the voice, raspy from cigars. I hung up the receiver and took a deep breath.

If Elisenda hadn't moved in with her parents after breaking up with me, if this was one of those times when, even though something couldn't be, it was, and Elisenda was with *another man*, then her parents would not, in all likelihood, have heard about our breakup, they wouldn't be aware of it, because you don't tell your parents these things right away, no matter how much you love them and trust them, and thus they wouldn't yet know that Elisenda had left me, and that I was now that loneliest number, one. And if, God forbid, that was the case, then I would certainly look foolish asking her father if she was there, since he, assuming she was at my place, wouldn't understand my reason for calling, and would start to ask questions, questions that would be too hard to answer. I decided then to camouflage my voice and pass myself off as someone else. I rolled up a towel around the receiver, a trick I've never understood but have seen in too many movies to not attempt now that I had a chance to do so, and dialed the Rius' number. "Hello, who's calling?" asked Señor Rius more impatiently this time. "Is Elisenda there?" I asked, lowering my voice. "Yes, hold on, I'll get her," he answered. Hearing those words filled me with euphoria. "What can't be, can't be, Grandma," I thought to myself as Elisenda's father went to find her, proving as he did so that the trick of putting the towel over the receiver only works in movies: he shouted that it was me on the line.

I won't transcribe here my conversation with Elisenda, for the content was predictable and the transcription therefore unnecessary. I do wish to note, however, that the soft voice with which she spoke sounded as sweet and melodious to my ears as the murmur of the surf at dusk; that I imagined her sitting on her father's sofa in a long black velvet skirt and a low-cut beige blouse, which, together with the blond hair spilling over her shoulders, made me think, I don't know why, of the nineteenth century; that while we spoke I finally confirmed something I only suspected before hearing her voice, which was that as soon as I registered that Elisenda had really left me, I'd begun to love her again as I loved her before, in those first weeks or months after I met her; that I therefore felt drawn once more by a hidden, mysterious force, by those powerful depths where my happiness peacefully dozed; that I didn't realize then how frail and ridiculous a man can be, and if someone had tried to butt into our conversation and point this out, I would have let him have it; that I insisted we had to talk about things in person; and that in the end, not without a certain show of reluctance, she agreed to see me that very afternoon.

The place chosen (by Elisenda) for our meeting was a park located two blocks from her parents' house, one of those dusty, dreadful squares full of dog droppings and adorned with a couple of sickly plants that the city insists on calling green spaces. We planned to meet at seven that evening, but I got there half an hour early to scout out the terrain and get into position. First I chose a bench next to the park entrance, I figured this way I'd have no trouble spotting her. Later, though, it occurred to me that I would do better to remain on foot, because, first, that way I could mask my nervousness (excess body movement is less justifiable and more visible when you're seated), and second, in the event that the conversation went well, very well, I felt that the hugging and kissing of making up would be easier, and more fitting, aesthetically, if performed in a vertical position. So I waited next to one of the four pine trees planted in the park, a gloomy, stunted pine in a lonely corner, deserted by all but a small dog that occasionally came by to bark at me. Nervous, I'd give the mutt a kick, and it would run off and disappear, but after a few minutes which it apparently spent preparing a counteroffensive, it would come back with renewed hostility; at one point it grabbed the cuff of my trousers and tried to bite my ankle with its tiny mouth.

Elisenda was late. Cigarette butts accumulated around the tree I had chosen to wait by. I even thought she wouldn't come, that she regretted agreeing to see me and decided at the last minute to stand me up. But she came. At seven eighteen I saw her arrive through one of the two entrances to the park. She looked around, trying to locate me. She wasn't wearing the black velvet skirt nor the beige blouse I imagined during our phone conversation, but that didn't matter: she looked even prettier in jeans and a pink T-shirt, a tight, short-sleeve T-shirt that outlined two sweet, round breasts, no longer the breasts I had caressed so many times, but rather surprisingly foreign breasts, banished from the realm of my possessions and graced with the allure of the unreachable.

I stayed where I was and waved my arms in the air to make myself visible. I was relieved to see her smile at me, though it was an instinctive smile, mere good manners. The kindness of formalities: even a heartless killer, if approached with politeness or urgency, would have a hard time not giving a passerby the time of day or a light for his cigarette. But we cling to whatever we need to for reassurance and encouragement, and we interpret the gestures of others in our favor. And so I felt the meeting had started off well, and that her smile was an open door, an invitation, and a change of heart. When she arrived she greeted me without a kiss, although this omission I ignored, unlike her smile. I asked how her parents were, and she replied dutifully, following my lead, not letting on that she knew I had no interest in family reports: once again the kindness of formalities, the formulas that serve as bridges to what really matters. "I'm glad they're well," I said, as if I hadn't heard from them in a long time, as if I hadn't had dinner with her parents four or five days earlier, when nothing had yet happened and my relationship with Elisenda was still invulnerable and everlasting. Of course, time measured by calendars and clocks isn't the same as the time we use to fix memories in our mind, and a lot of time had passed for me since that dinner. In the same way, I felt as though I hadn't seen Elisenda in months, when in reality, she had moved out not two days before.

But that wasn't quite it, it wasn't just that there was an unfathomable fissure between actual time and subjective time. Elisenda, too, had changed for me. No longer was she the same. I couldn't look at her in the same way. For the first time in years, Elisenda was once again someone distinct from me, separate from me, independent of me. Before my eyes, her figure recovered the *otherness* that living together had eventually erased. And I felt as though I had been given the chance to meet her again, to win her love, to love her as I loved her at the beginning. The promise renewed itself, and in her eyes there glowed again that potent, hidden region which I once wanted to make mine and had slowly, unconsciously, given up.

Sadly, though not coincidentally, my love revived just as I started to lose her, when it was perhaps too late to hold on to her.

"I told you the other day, I'm not sure I want to continue with our relationship. I need time to think," she replied when I asked her straightaway, point blank, to move back in. "Don't take it the wrong way. It's not that I don't love you," she went on. "It's just that sometimes, even if you love somebody very much, it's better for both people to have some space. And sometimes it's hard to understand, and it's tough, but it's better that way. At least for a while. So that we can sort through our feelings, see the relationship from another angle," she said, and though neither her words nor her tone were harsh or categorical, though she didn't present the breakup as something permanent, I realized Elisenda would never come back to me. And then I, who had fashioned arguments and memorized brilliant phrases over the three quarters of an hour I spent waiting for her, and even planned to tell her about my problem with Señora Ruscarons to make her take pity on me, and thus change her mind, leaned back on the tree trunk and remained silent. "Don't you have anything to say?" she asked, placing her hand on my arm like a caring mother. And I shrugged and said nothing, like a child who still has no response to the cruelties of the world and wants his mother to answer for him. And suddenly the mutt reappeared, though now it didn't bark, or maybe it did and I didn't notice. It darted between us and jumped up with its legs forward. Elisenda bent down and reached out to the dog, as though wanting to cradle it in her arms. "Good boy, yes! Come to mama," she said, and the dog ran up to her, wagging its tail, lifting its two front legs so Elisenda could grab them. "You want to play, don't you? Aren't you a playful little doggy? Yes you are!" she laughed. "What a cutie! Look how he lifts up his legs!" she kept saying, raising her eyes to meet mine with a carefree smile, as though she'd already forgotten what were we talking about, as though she didn't recall breaking up with me once and for all and didn't stop to think that this would probably be the last time we'd see each other in these circumstances, with the intimacy and closeness of a relationship which, now doomed, nevertheless prolonged its existence for a few more minutes. And I forced a half-smile and thought about how sad it is when two people say good-bye but don't know or don't want to know that they're saying good-bye, and act as if there were nothing the matter, without the solemnity which the situation requires, and which could at least mitigate the awkwardness. And with bitter resignation I told myself that after this evening there would be no more evenings spent with Elisenda, there would be no more parks for us to meet at, or dogs running around at our feet while Elisenda lifted up her green eyes to my puzzled eyes to say, in her soft, velvet voice: "Don't you love him? Isn't he just the cutest?" And I was overcome by a ruthless nostalgia for the whole scene, for those last moments which, even as they signaled our final separation, still belonged to both of us, still embraced us as the couple we no longer were, still made it possible for a distracted passerby, for example, to look at us briefly and assume we were together, as boyfriend and girlfriend, or husband and wife, or lovers seeking refuge in a dark, secluded corner of the park. Just as that present became the past, a past I was already starting to miss, the future appeared momentarily in the sight of Elisenda playing with the dog. And that nostalgia and sadness then merged with all the angst of a jeopardized, increasingly uncertain future, and I felt as though the entire park, broken off from the rest of the earth by a minor tremor that left intact the patch of ground where I stood, now began to spin vertiginously around me. Dizzy, I slid my back down the tree trunk and sat on the ground with my knees bent. "Are you all right? What's the matter?" Elisenda asked, her words suddenly stopping the spinning of the park. "I'm fine, don't worry, I just got a little dizzy," I answered, looking through my jacket for my pack of cigarettes.

7

THAT SAME EVENING, when I returned home, I called Maserachs to ask if he'd be willing to take over my work at the office for the following week. At that time of year there wouldn't be very much, anyway: a few appointments, a couple of wrongful termination disputes, the draft of a lawsuit that Maserachs himself had passed on to me. He responded to my request with predictable surprise, as well as his usual string of expletives, but in the end, just as I expected, he agreed.

Maserachs had always considered me a rival. We joined Santasusana's firm at more or less the same time, and from the very start he viewed our relationship as a competition to see who would be Santasusana's favorite. Luckily (or unluckily), Santasusana wasn't one to play favorites or rank his associates, but nevertheless Maserachs tried at every turn to prove his greater worth. And to do so he resorted to the most convoluted tricks, which occasionally verged on the ridiculous. For instance, if we arrived at the same time in the morning and were both looking for a parking spot near the office, Maserachs, in order to get to work first, and thus show Santasusana that he was more punctual and more of a go-getter than I was, would double-park in front of the building, go in, say good morning to Santasusana and pretend to shut himself up in his office, only to leave again right away, on the sly or under some pretense, to go park the car correctly; if we took the same elevator or ran into each other at the front door, Maserachs pretended not to have seen me outside, and even had the nerve to greet me with a certain severity, as though reproaching me for my tardiness. His competitive spirit was so childish and pathetic that it annoyed me only at first. Later on, I discovered that Maserachs's unchecked ambition could be a convenient ally, a subtle way to get out of the tasks I found most burdensome or disagreeable, since my dedicated coworker would take them on with proud condescension. Thus I gradually managed to spend less time at oral hearings, which always filled me with an overwhelming dread, and to focus on more pleasant, innocuous tasks like drawing up lawsuits or wrongful termination cases, a task at which Maserachs, incidentally, was totally hopeless. I knew well, in short, that every time I gave up he regarded it as a victory. So I wasn't surprised that afternoon when, after telling me how "unprofessional" my behavior was, he ultimately said, in his pinched, shrill voice: "Fine. If necessary, I shall assume responsibility for your duties."

I hung up and smiled with satisfaction. The first hurdle was behind me. I picked up the receiver again and dialed Santasusana's number. I did so without much thought, once again taking the plunge.

It's not nice to let down someone who sympathizes with us, who forgives us in advance; no, I don't like letting Santasusana down, I don't want him to think I'm a coward who turns tail at the first scent of danger. I don't like coming up short and letting him see my weakness and my cowardice, but my fingers are already dialing his phone number, and I hear his voice, and it truly is painful to say what I'm about to say, that I won't be at work that week, I'm going away for a few days, I can't take the pressure. It's really difficult but there's no going back, my brain has given the order and my lips are about to start moving to say what they have to say. But in the meantime it's Santasusana who's speaking, he tells me about his conversation with Señora Ruscarons: "of course I told her we'd cover the amount she lost for our mistake (he says our mistake, not your mistake), but you know how stubborn she is, she says that now it's a question of honor and justice, and she doesn't like being jerked around, and soon we'll see, we don't know who we're dealing with." All this Santasusana says Señora Ruscarons said, and it's painful and humiliating to have to tell him this now, but my lips have been set in motion and say it: "Well, look, it's not just because of the wrongful termination hearing, though of course that's had an

effect on me and I feel terrible about it, but all that unpleasant-
ness aside, I'm going through a rough time, and . . . well, just
like you suggested . . . I mean, I think maybe it wouldn't be a bad
idea if I did take a few days off, maybe that way I can sort out
this issue, which, recently . . . well, that's why I haven't been as
focused on my work as I should be . . . and I want to get it sorted
out as soon as possible, it's a rather delicate matter . . . I mean,
nothing serious, but delicate, and the whole thing with Señora
Ruscarons . . . well, it's made me realize I have to do something,
I don't want my personal issues to interfere with my work . . . I
mean, oversights like the one that happened the other day are
inexcusable, and I take full responsibility, and that's why . . ."
And the words continue to spout unstoppably from my mouth
because there's no one to control them: I've stepped aside, and
it's as though I'm not the one talking, and my voice won't stop
even when Santasusana tries to say something.

"Hold on," he says, but I keep hearing my own voice: "And
since I talked to Maserachs and he says he doesn't mind . . . and
since as you know this time of year the workload is pretty light
. . ."

And Santasusana's voice returns, this time more forcefully.
"Hold on, listen," he says, and at last, to my surprise, I hear the
words stop coming out of my mouth, at last I feel the mechanism
inside me generating them cease all at once, the way pulling the
plug makes the cassette suddenly stop. "Hold on, listen, you
have nothing to explain. That sounds like a wise decision. Take
as many days as you need. Ricardo and I will cover your work
between the two of us. You have to take care of what matters, and
right now what matters is for you to make sure you're all right.
And of course, you can count on me for anything you need—
you know that, right? All you have to do is call, for anything,
hear me? Anything at all . . . And as for Señora Ruscarons, don't
you worry about her, you've got the full support of the firm. It'll
blow over, it's not such a big deal, at most you'll get a warning
from the Bar Association, but they're on your side, don't forget
that, so there's nothing to worry about, you hear me? Hear me?"
Yes, I hear him, but his words have touched me and I can't get

the autopilot working again. "Hello? Are you there? Can you hear me?"

"That's very kind of you," I finally manage to say, in a faltering voice, and now I'm the one talking. "I'm really sorry I've gotten you tangled up in this, I can't thank you enough for your support and understanding, I wish I knew how to make it up to you."

"The only thing you have to do for me is focus on those issues of yours, once you've got them sorted out and are back in the office, Maserachs and I will find a way to make you pay for all the work you made us do, don't worry about that," he says, joking, despite the fact that Santasusana isn't one for jokes.

"No, seriously—I really appreciate it."

"Don't mention it, and don't hesitate to call me if there's anything you need, understand? Anything at all."

When I hung up I felt a twinge in my heart, a twinge of tenderness, melancholy, self-pity, regret—who knows what I felt just then. Whatever it was, tears clouded my eyes for the second time in just a few hours and I felt my life pushing deeper and deeper into a maze of confusion and sadness.

I went to my room, opened my dresser, grabbed some clothes at random: some shirts, some pairs of underwear, some socks, a second pair of trousers, and stuffed them all in my travel bag.

I went back to the living room. It was nine thirty-five. I phoned Alberto and the answering machine picked up. I waited for the sound of the beep and left the following message: "Alberto, I'm going out of town for a few days. Not long, a week at most. I wanted to let you know since we said we'd be in touch . . . Anyway, didn't want you to be surprised if you couldn't reach me. I need a few days to get some thinking done." (The phrase sounded extremely sappy, but I liked it). "See you when I get back. If I can, I'll call you one day from wherever I am, though I still don't know where that will be. Talk to you soon."

I hung up and glanced around the room. It's surprising how much of a mess a man can make in just two days. In just two days, during which I had hardly even set foot in the apartment, the place had been turned upside down. I thought it wouldn't be a bad idea to have the cleaning lady come, but Elisenda always took care of that, she was the one who called her whenever she thought we needed it. I didn't have her number, and would have felt incapable of calling her even if I did. I shrugged in resignation, or perhaps trusting that, upon my return, I would miraculously find the place clean and tidy. I bent down, picked up my travel bag and left my apartment.

Confusion is powerlessness before the intensity of feeling. It's our inability to take command of our minds with sufficient authority to organize our feelings and give them, through thought, a framework that can encompass and explain them, make them compatible with reality. That's how I felt as I left that hostile city in a rush and under cover of darkness: incapable of assuming power within myself, at the mercy of a whirlwind of untamable feelings.

Through the car window, as I drove away, the city showed me a hateful and menacing face, like the face of someone who saw you commit a crime and is threatening you with blackmail. Invisible eyes peered at me from every corner with malicious intent, giving me to know there was conclusive evidence against me. My confusion had rendered all bridges to reality unpassable, all save one: guilt. I felt guilty, guilty of everything and nothing in particular, like when you're convinced you forgot something important and can't recall exactly what.

I drove quickly, eager to lose sight of the city, like a criminal running away to start a peaceful, orderly new life far from the pain that caused his misdeeds. Unfortunately, I'm a poor driver and on two occasions almost crashed: first into a plastic garbage container, then later into a van that came out unexpectedly on my right. I tried to calm down. I tried to come up with a plan. I tried to differentiate my feelings and put them in some kind of order.

I had only partly succeeded when I found myself driving through outlying neighborhoods that no longer looked familiar: long avenues and imposing blocks that offered me the reassuring protection of anonymity. Then I lit a cigarette and slowed down. I switched on the radio, but hearing the theme song for the news, I switched it off again. I breathed a sigh of relief when I saw the sign for the expressway; it had been months since I'd left Barcelona by car and I didn't have it all together.

I got on the expressway. The city, wrapped in a shimmering fog, grew smaller in the rearview mirror. In the opposite direction there were more than a few cars on the road, lured no doubt by the promise of a Saturday night on the town, but the northbound side had minimal traffic, only an occasional vehicle speeding past me and quickly vanishing into a distant, fading point of light.

I drove barely twenty kilometers, after which I got off the expressway and pulled up at a roadside hotel. Years back, after an unfortunately timed breakdown, I had been forced to spend the night there while I waited for the repair shop to open. This time, however, my stop was planned. Since I dislike driving at night but couldn't stand the thought of spending another hour in Barcelona, I decided to stay in that ratty hotel on the outskirts of the city and drive on the next day.

I couldn't fall asleep for a long time, but eventually my eyes closed and I slept eight hours straight. In the morning, on my way out, I stopped by a highway map hanging on one of the lobby walls. I was looking for a destination, any destination that would spare me the constant indecision of drifting. Running my finger along the red line that indicated a provincial highway, I suddenly happened upon a name I didn't expect to see. The name resounded inside me as I read it and sparked an extremely potent current, a force that all at once cleared away the lingering muddle from the night before and seemed suddenly to concentrate my dispersed, floating, chaotic feelings into a single channel. Sant Honorat de Valldonzella was the name. I suddenly felt an overwhelming desire to feel nostalgic, to get drunk on the past, to lose sight of the present. I paid the hotel bill and set off.

8

EARLY ON, BY age six or seven, I started to sense that something odd and suspicious happened to the past. I always found it strange that the times I remembered seemed so much happier than my life at the moment. For a while this impression (that the past was always better than the present) even led me to think that life would always get worse, go downhill, a proposition that caused me considerable distress. Eventually, however, I started to realize that the happiness of past moments did not necessarily stand in direct proportion to the amount of time gone by since I experienced them; an afternoon spent at the movies two weeks back, for example, might strike me as more extraordinary than the morning I had gone fishing with my uncle three years earlier, and this fact seemed incompatible with the notion of a progressive and constant decline.

In this way I began to concede the possibility that the aura of happiness enveloping the past had never really existed. That is, the greater affection I felt for past experiences did not perhaps mean they were objectively better than the ones I was having as I recalled them, but stemmed from something added later, after they had moved outside the core of the present, like an unseen hand that redecorates the scene when the show is over and the actors have left the theater. Could this be? Could it be that moments from the past, once they were no longer present, underwent a process of embellishment and appeared to me later enhanced by a light and a charm they lacked when I experienced them?

One afternoon when I went with my mother to the market I hit upon a way to uncover, I thought, what was really happening with the passage of time. My mother was holding my hand and we were walking slowly, stopping in front of the displays. There was nothing out of the ordinary about that afternoon: I didn't feel especially happy, and in fact I was annoyed and a little sad that my mother had refused to buy me some candy at the kiosk. Suddenly I began to wonder whether I would, in time, wistfully remember even this insignificant and rather sad moment. When we stopped in front of a florist's, I carefully studied the various flowers, I inhaled their perfume, I noted the sign that read "Freixas Flowers" in green letters on an orange background, and I concentrated and tried to record that moment in my memory. When I opened my eyes again I said, "If later on, when I look back on this gray afternoon, it appears as a bright, happy experience, then I'll know that time turns reality into something false and that I can never trust my memories."

Of course, the experiment was doomed to failure. The passage of time admits no meddling or counsel in its selection of experiences to be crystallized and recalled in the future. We're not allowed to decide which moments will join our past and which will hide their faces as though they had never existed. Everyone's mosaic of remembered history lies beyond personal choice. True, by concentrating all my attention, I managed to retain that specific scene in my memory (along with the whole trip with my mother), and I could therefore look back on it whenever I pleased; however, I failed to take into account a key factor that nullified the whole experiment: by consciously using that moment, by turning it into the object of my investigation, I prevented it from completing its natural journey to the past, or kept it indefinitely in the present, which amounts to the same thing. The trip with my mother now formed part of an experiment that extended into the future. So a few months later, when I recalled the image of myself standing in front of Freixas Flowers, what I saw was not a photograph from the past but a scene still playing out in the present and therefore free from any nostalgia, immune to the process of embellishment that I hoped to unmask. Frustrated by the results of my investigation, I undertook new experiments, held onto other experiences and analyzed time's later effects on them, but always with the same result:

they all seemed immune to nostalgia. I constantly fell victim, however, to unexpected bouts of nostalgia, nostalgia for things I hadn't paid attention to as they occurred, things I hadn't tried to retain and thought I'd forgotten, but which suddenly, when I heard a tune or a word, when I caught a scent or happened upon some scenery, revived again spontaneously, with unsuspected strength and splendor. Since I couldn't recall what they had been like in the present, those moments added nothing to my investigation. I felt like the castle guard who waits impatiently by the trap he's devised while the enemies sneak in through the other side of the fortress. I grew increasingly convinced that time had an invisible hand tasked with dressing up experiences once they left the bounds of the present, but I couldn't manage to prove the existence of that mysterious process.

But the years went by, and then one morning, when I was fourteen or fifteen and had long since forgotten those experiments, I walked by a flower stand in a hospital lobby. Suddenly, the lobby vanished in a blinding flash, as if a crowd of photographers had all pointed their cameras at me and begun to shoot, and there emerged before me, in fragmentary images linked by a single, intense perfume, the memory of that distant afternoon. Then I was seized by nostalgia. I think I even stopped for a moment and closed my eyes, trying to feel that intensely bittersweet sensation to the fullest. At last my experiment from long ago produced results that confirmed my suspicions; at last that humdrum afternoon appeared before me like something delightful and unrepeatable. I cut off the nostalgia growing inside me, and when all my senses had returned to the present, I smiled in satisfaction and pride.

Contrary to what people usually think, no time is quite so weighed down by nostalgia as childhood. Changes come so swiftly that there's no time for children to form a complete picture of the successive worlds they inhabit. No sooner has a child adapted to one state of affairs than a new transformation comes and rearranges the set. And so, in a rush, with no time for mourning or good-byes, pulled along by the voracity of events, children leave behind the scenery that welcomed them, the still-unfinished worlds that are gone before they've wholly grasped them, worlds made up of a multitude of images, smells, sounds, impressions; worlds which, once lost, will begin to emit signals from far away, spanning time and reaching the present with all the magic and beauty of a familiar tune, demanding that they return. I wanted to cover my ears, to block out that sirens' chorus. Just as the whirlwind of changes left lost, orphaned paradises in its wake, it opened up, in the opposite direction, a luminous space that now sought to overpower me. My expectations for the future, for a scarcely explored, almost infinite, still-virgin future, dragged me forward and drove me to break the chains of my past. And now at last I had the proof I needed, the argument that would let me resolve, in favor of the future, the contradiction inside me between the pain of loss and my desire to grow: nostalgia, which had so often filled me with melancholy, was nothing but a shameful capitulation to the illusions of time; memory was nothing but a distortion of the real experience that once served as its frame. Why should we feel nostalgia for something that never existed as we remember it? Why should we want to return to a time whose only image we possess is false, unreal? Why remain stuck in a past that in truth does not belong to us?

But the years go by, we grow up, become adults, and as the volume of our experiences increases, the space we allot to the future grows proportionally smaller. The play of lights created by the various planes of time always changes, just as spotlights offer different views of a hall as their brightness is adjusted. Our former concept of time will no longer do, and we have to find another that fits the circumstances and better aligns with our current needs. As a child I devised an experiment to help shield me from the past, and now, oddly enough, at thirty-three, with an insatiable thirst for nostalgia, that same experiment led me to draw very different conclusions, and to justify my journey back to those lost years.

To experience the present, we have a limited number of senses available, all of which arise from a state of urgency. A moviegoer has access to a much richer and more complex world than the film's characters, who are excessively, almost pornographically involved in the action, and therefore can't pay attention to what's around them, can't watch themselves move through the story. The same thing happens with our own experiences. Just as when we cross a narrow, rickety bridge, our eyes ignore the view and search for the precise spot we have to set our foot so as not to tumble into the abyss, when we move through the present our perception is likewise limited to the sensory link between the moment we're in and the one immediately following. That's why, as I walked alongside my mother that afternoon, my senses could perceive only what was closest to me, what was most viscerally and directly involved in what I was doing: the fatigue in my legs, the sound of a car horn that made me turn toward the street, a breeze that picked up suddenly and made the hair on my arms stand on end, a group of children running after a ball who made us slow down, the disappointment and anger at my mother for refusing to buy me those candies at the kiosk . . . The context around that experience, however, remained excluded from the present moment. In order for my senses to perceive it, that context would have to be constantly renewed, and would have to create a stimulus intense enough to compete with the attention demanded by everything else around me. Strolling with my mother, for instance, was no doubt a pleasant, enjoyable activity, but also a habitual one, almost routine at that time, so that the pleasure of the stroll, lacking in novelty, was subordinated to the contingencies of the present: it could be ruined by some slight physical discomfort or a sudden upsetting of the routine. In the same way, the set of underlying circumstances in my life at the time, without which that afternoon would have become something totally different, could not, as I progressed through that present, reach the surface of perception. The closeness that bound me to my mother, my absence of anxiety about the future, the budding attraction I felt to a girl from school, the tune I constantly hummed, the privileges and preoccupations unique to childhood . . . all these floated in the air that afternoon but passed by me wholly unnoticed. My experience was limited to a group of mostly dull, everyday sensations, and based on these I concluded that the afternoon would never deserve to be missed; if I ever looked back on it with nostalgia, therefore, it could only be because reality itself had been falsified.

I was mistaken. Simple minds tend to grant the present a monopoly on the real, but only when we regard reality from afar does it shows us all of its faces, only from the past does reality open all its doors to our senses, and only then can we discover the meaning that a certain experience had for us. For we grasp the complete world of sensations underlying a certain situation only once that situation's protagonist has become, with the passage of time, someone different from the self who's remembering. We have to step out of our own life to appreciate it, to discover the substrate it rests on, to recover all the intensity of those sensations which, blocked by urgency, we couldn't experience in the moment.

Yes, an intense nostalgia swept over me as I walked past the flower stand in the hospital lobby. For at last that distant afternoon I'd tried to hold onto had irrevocably become part of the past. I was leaving childhood behind and entering adolescence. The world had changed around me and other laws governed my life. My mother's work obligations had caused those strolls to vanish from my life, and even if, exceptionally, I might still have the chance to go on a walk with her, that walk would now be something wholly different, because I too had changed, I too had become someone else, someone who, for example, thought he was too old to complain about candy or have his mother hold his hand. And it was for that very reason—because I had become someone else and was no longer a child, and no longer had the chance to repeat that stroll in the present—that the memory brought me a wealth of sensations from my past. The child walking in my memory was no longer subject to the limitations of the present, he had within his grasp the thrilling possibility of feeling it all at the same time, the whole word of impressions which nourished my life back then. And that child, who was no

longer me but remained bound to me by an ambiguous bond
of sameness, let me share with him (though I resisted his gift,
convinced it was an illusion), for a few seconds, that intoxicating,
overpowering mixture of sensations that were both essence and
metaphor of a lost era.

I thought about all this now, as I drove down the winding highway toward Sant Honorat. I was set on recovering my past, I
wanted to reconnect with the boy who lived in that town years
ago, and I had the feeling that if I succeeded, if I managed to
rekindle inside me some of the happiness the town had given
me as a child, I could face the future with renewed strength. The
person I thought I was until a few days before had now begun
to disappear, and the prospect of facing my future without the
armor that my identity used to provide sent me reeling in terror.
But there stood my past to remind me that all was not lost, that
not everything had been engulfed by the devastating, ravenous
void, that some part of me still remained, something tough and
incorruptible, something full of life which, after lying dormant
all those years, would now awaken to welcome me into its arms
and save me from the fall.

The morning was blue and warm. I drove down the middle of
the narrow highway with one arm out the window, occasionally
raising it to feel the wind's resistance or tapping to the beat of the
music I found on the radio. The dense oak forests that ran along
the road soon gave way to wide green fields unexpectedly dotted
with poppies and daisies. I recognized some of the farmhouses,
as well as the remains of a castle atop a little hill where we often
went to picnic among the ruins. The harmony permeating the
environment of the morning seemed to become more perfect
and intense the closer I came to my destination, but also more
fragile and delicate. My movements, as I lit a cigarette, changed
gears, or turned the wheel, were slow and deliberate. The sun
shone higher and higher in the sky.

After a sharp curve, I spotted some blocks of three- and

four-story buildings in the distance, at the end of a straight
stretch approximately two kilometers long. Behind them were
hints of other, shorter buildings in the shadows.

9

I PARKED THE car at the entrance to the town and walked the two remaining blocks to the Hotel San Remo. Years ago, if you arrived at the town from the provincial highway, this hotel was the first building you saw.

I reserved a room and let them know I'd be back in a couple of hours. The manager, stepping out from behind the counter and standing behind me, stopped me as I headed toward the door.

"Is this your first time at the hotel?" he asked, ending the sentence in an almost unintelligible whisper, as though he realized too late he may have committed an indiscretion.

"Yes, it's my first time," I said, relieved that he didn't recognize me.

It was a half-lie. It was in fact my first time staying at the hotel. However, I had been there many times, tagging along with my father, who was once in the habit of taking his Sunday aperitif at the hotel bar.

"Oh—my mistake," he said. "I was certain I'd seen you here before."

The manager's name was Ernest and he was the son of the owner, though perhaps his father had died and now he owned the hotel. He was two years older than I and had a huge birthmark on his back. Even as a child, when I met him, you could tell at first glance he was destined to be the town fool. This fact made him the butt of all our cruelties. "Poor Ernest, we were so mean to you," I thought as he looked at me, mouth agape, waiting for a smile, for some reassuring word from his new guest. He had filled out, especially around his face. His fleshy jowls imprisoned his thin lips and reduced his chin to a small greasy ball.

"Well, I must have a pretty run-of-the-mill face," I joked.

My words seemed to relieve Ernest, who had remained quite still awaiting my response and now burst out laughing, waving a kitchen towel in the air.

"Don't say that, sir, it's not true. It's just that since I see so many people coming through here, I end up feeling like I should know everybody."

I wandered for an hour through the town. I walked down every street, revisited all the old spots. I hardly recognized a thing. New three- and four-story buildings altered the town's profile and at every turn I found new storefronts and shops that were no different from the ones in the city. Even the townspeople, once so rural, seemed to have stepped straight off of Barcelona's Paseo de Gracia. The church bell tower, which years ago stood out sharply against the sky and helped absentminded wanderers quickly get their bearings, was now hidden behind all the concrete. In the plaza, across from city hall, they had put in a huge Caprabo supermarket.

What surprises us most when we return somewhere after a long absence isn't so much the inevitable changes we encounter, but the realization (made visible in those changes) that life continued its course after we left, that the world didn't stop with our departure. And we're seized by a sense of having been wronged, like a property owner whose rights have been infringed upon. What infuriates and puzzles us is not so much the transformations we discover as the fact that they took place without our knowledge, behind our backs, for we assumed that since our mental picture of the place hadn't changed, it remained practically intact, nearly identical to how we left it. And although reason tries to resist such an egocentric view, and we tell ourselves it's normal for things to change with time, until we readjust to the new landscape we can't help feeling betrayed.

Sad and disgruntled, I even entertained the idea of changing plans and leaving this town, but gradually my initial irritation gave way to indifference, and I told myself that I had nowhere better to go anyway.

Over the following three days I barely left the hotel. I'd sleep until two or three in the afternoon and then hurry downstairs to get something to eat in the restaurant before the kitchen closed. Then I'd go back to my room, and after taking a shower and making myself halfway presentable, come down to the restaurant again, which at that time of day served as a café. I'd spend the rest of the afternoon there, reading a newspaper, having a soft drink and waiting until dinnertime. At night I'd shut myself in my room and let the hours slip by, doing nothing. Not once during those the three days did I manage to get to sleep before dawn.

Even so, I didn't feel bad. By the second day I felt as though I'd spent a long time in the hotel. I had settled into a pleasant transitory state that kept all worries at bay. My life in Barcelona, with all its troubles and obligations and sorrows, seemed distant, indefinitely postponed. In fact, I didn't feel any responsibility or obligation tying me to that life, and while sooner or later someone would have to sort out the situation, that someone, I felt, wasn't me.

True, in Sant Honorat I didn't find what I had come looking for, but the refuge which the past seemed to deny me I found in being a guest. In the Hotel San Remo life was organized around a comfortable, simple routine that required nothing of me but sufficient money to pay the bills. There were no demands, no duties, no judgments of any kind. Ernest took care of me; at every moment he went out of his way to do me small kindnesses, which I accepted only so as not to disappoint him. My interactions with the rest of the guests, most of them business travelers, were polite and discreet; we said hello in the restaurant or made an occasional comment about the weather. There were no suspicious glances, no menacing stares. Everything was smooth and easy, free of hassles or problems. I saw myself simply as another guest at the hotel, giving no more thought to my existence. This new trouble-free life, this new linear, sharply defined identity, came out to seven thousand six hundred pesetas per day, board included. Those days were peaceful, even happy, but something told me I was deluding myself.

It seems logical, predictable, that we should drink deep in nostalgia when we return to the setting of a happy childhood; it's to be expected that, as we step into one of memory's sacred places, a torrent of feelings and reminiscences will pour out, leaving us floating in a cottony, ethereal reality. But we almost never feel what we ought to feel. We're constantly surprised by distorted, insufficient, improper emotions: the man who attends his best friend's funeral and can't find a sincere enough sorrow inside; the mother who sees her son after twenty years of exile and is surprised by her own coldness and indifference; the good Samaritan who saves the life of someone in need and doesn't quite feel the satisfaction he thought himself entitled to; the child who opens her presents on Christmas Day and can't manage to shake off an inexplicable boredom. In the case of those who are unspontaneous by nature, as I am, the situation is more extreme. Our intelligence follows quicker, simpler paths than our emotions, and when it reaches reality the emotions aren't yet there to back it up. That's why most of our emotions are the product of a simulation, a mere pretense. We know what we ought to feel, and want to feel, but the emotion hasn't quite reached us. And so, as if imitating the call of a bird to beckon it onto our hand, we imagine the feelings we deem appropriate. We pretend to feel so that our feelings become genuine. And we adopt the pose and hollow out our soul, and by virtue of our belief in our own performance, a true emotion eventually wells up.

Although I chose to return out of a need to feel nostalgia, a need to feel protected from the harsh present by the gentleness of the past, the fact is that in the four days I'd spent there, Sant Honorat de Valldonzella had not succeeded in awakening any of the emotions I hoped to find. A voice inside me, however, reminded me I still had unfinished business.

On the fifth day, early in the afternoon, since a northerly wind had picked up and the heat had slightly subsided, I decided to end my confinement and go out for a ride. I asked Ernest if he could lend me a bicycle, and, blushing, he offered me a rickety BH we found in the storeroom.

I got on and rode a few laps around the storeroom under Ernest's watchful eye. At first I almost lost my balance, but once I picked up speed, I steadied myself on the bicycle. I let go with one hand and waved good-bye.

"Will you be dining at the hotel?" he yelled after me.

"I think so, Ernest, I think so," I called back.

The road follows a slight rise over wheat fields and wild meadows, and after a long bend loses sight of the town and descends into a lush, humid valley where a row of cypresses partly conceals the house that belonged to my family. Further on, the road runs parallel to a stream and then forks into two more paths that pick their way through country houses and poultry farms, before disappearing behind the mountain that looms over the horizon.

Unlike the town, the landscape I now surveyed before descending the slope that would lead me into the valley had hardly undergone any changes. The same colors were still there, the same shapes, the same houses, even the same scent from the wheat fields.

I released the hand brake and coasted down the path until I reached the house, which was surrounded by a green metal fence poorly masked by roses and other bushes. A four-by-four parked in the yard partly obscured the front door. Thick smoke issued from the chimney, but the dining room curtains were drawn shut.

I set the bicycle against a lone withered chestnut tree on the side of the road and began walking slowly toward the house. "I haven't been here in over fifteen years," I said to myself, and I searched my mind for some image of the past that could frame this encounter. And though no specific memory came to

my aid then, as I approached the fence around the yard I felt
that the present was fading around me, and that in its place
a blurry reality emerged, made up of a jumbled succession
of stimuli that were strangely familiar but not wholly recognizable. I veered a little to the right, just enough to reach an
angle from which I could see, despite the irritating presence
of the all-terrain vehicle, the front door to the house. At first
I thought it had been changed, or at least that the door had
been repainted, its original brown softened by a layer of beige,
but after a second I was no longer so sure: I couldn't swear that
the door I saw wasn't exactly the same as it had been years
before, when my family owned the house. But then, notic-
ing a small object at the foot of the door, I looked down and
discovered a metal container of the kind used to hold milk.
And the vision of that metal jug, slightly rounded in the belly,
with a lid shaped like a Tyrolean hat, threw me back into the
past so powerfully that I didn't need to force the images and
couldn't have contained them if I'd tried. Until that moment
my memory had been working intermittently, like a radio with
patchy reception, catching fleeting bursts that couldn't form
a prolonged, coherent scene, but as soon as I saw the milk jug
I suddenly felt I had entered a captivating world, one I was
in no danger of being thrown out of, despite having just been
thrown in a moment before. The memories appeared swiftly,
but in precise detail, merging into one another seamlessly
and without interruption, holding me back from the present.
Suddenly I was sitting in the kitchen again, having breakfast,
overpowered by the scent of toast, drinking hot chocolate out
of a huge orange mug and hearing my sister's voice, far off,
probably in the pool, calling to my mother, and suddenly it
was me in the pool, intoxicated by an intense smell of chlorine
and freshly watered grass, and as I thought of the lawn I found
myself running through the yard, perhaps playing ball with
my friend Pablo, ignoring my mother, who stood on the porch
calling us in for snack time, and then suddenly I was by the
fireplace, watching the rain through the windowpanes while
behind me my father turned the pages of his newspaper. And I

felt the tedium and resigned anxiety of Sunday evenings, when it began to get dark and we had to get ready to head back to the city, or the thrill of diving headfirst into the pool's silvery water on full-moon nights, or the nervous excitement on days when we were expecting guests. And while my memory leapt from place to place, from scene to scene, the sensations lingered until long after the specific image that sparked them had disappeared, and blended the way colors blend and borders blur in an impressionist watercolor.

I don't know how long I was under the spell. In fact, as I revisited my memories I lost all sense of time. Perhaps it had been a quarter of an hour, perhaps only a few minutes. I didn't even notice that a storm was approaching, black clouds now covered the sky, and the sun could barely find a gap, a tiny sliver for its rays to poke through.

Only a violent clap of thunder brought me back to the present. But just as when you wake with a start, your dreams sometimes linger a while, twitching in your mind like a lizard's tail separated from the rest of its body, and you open your eyes and face the reality of the room with the aftertaste of the interrupted dream, so too the taste of the past remained within me even as I returned to the present. And with that same aftertaste I set out back to the hotel, pedaling under a torrential downpour, barely making out the ground I was riding over, with that thrill of velocity and risk so congenial to adolescence which now, catching me in full adulthood, blurred the borders of time and made me more certain by the minute that it was my eleven-year-old self who was riding through the rain. And then everything began to seem glorious, and my accelerated breathing was diluted in the thunderous drumming of the rain on the dry fields, while in the landscape rolling alongside me I caught glimmers of a powerful, long-standing affinity.

"Good lord!" exclaimed Ernest when he saw me walk dripping into the hotel lobby, skin plastered with soaked clothes and face streaming with drops as big as olives. "What on earth happened to you?"

"I got drenched," I answered, barely containing my excitement.

"Go up to your room this instant and get out of those wet clothes," he ordered, pointing to the staircase. "Meanwhile, I'll have them send up an herbal tea so you don't catch cold."

I stood there looking him up and down, stunned by the tenderness that this man inspired, remembering the cruel, heartless treatment my friends and I subjected him to when we were children.

"I mean, if you'd like, that is," he stammered.

"Of course, of course. Though if it's all the same to you"—I addressed him casually informally—"I'll take a rain check on the herbal tea. Right now I think what I need is some cognac," I added, heading up the stairs to the rooms.

I found myself floating between the past and the present, drawing on the essence of both, letting them mingle and merge.

As I changed clothes, the mirror reflected the image of a middle-aged man, but inside me pulsed impressions which, though filtered through the sense apparatus of an adult, reached me from childhood.

A strange euphoria had come over me, a joyful sensation of plenitude and harmony, and at last I felt that my life made sense again, and that I was again someone recognizable to myself. But I also felt that at any moment the mirage might vanish, at any moment I might fall back into the void, just as a drug addict falls victim to his own body once the effects of the drugs he's taken have worn off. How much longer could I revel in that state of grace? Could I hold on to some indelible imprint of that afternoon, some fortitude that would let me face the bleak future that awaited me back in Barcelona? Now that I had revisited my past, could I find room in my luggage for some token from my childhood, some identifying mark that would keep me connected to my own history?

Everything seemed too fragile. Like when someone gives us a phone number and we know that, if we don't keep repeating it until we can write it down in a planner, we'll soon forget it. How much longer would my memory hold out? And above all: how long could my senses remain attuned and receptive to the signals from the past?

Suddenly I felt an overwhelming desire to talk to my mother, to share my nostalgia with her, as if doing so would instill some solidity, some lasting quality into my memories. And I remembered the meetings my grandfather would organize with his old comrades in arms: that anxiety on the face of anyone who reminisced aloud about some episode, and turned to the others for confirmation, as if only by verifying that others recalled it, too, could they be certain that it actually occurred, as if the past could only be propped up by several people together, and would collapse and disintegrate if it dwelled in the memory of just one of them. I too felt the need to make my past bilateral, to offer it a means to communion with a memory that wasn't mine.

As soon as I got dressed and combed my hair, I went down to the café. Erminia, one of the servers, was stationed behind the bar and just about to pour the cognac carefully into a glass. In one corner of the room, a blond man, some forty years old, was sitting down to dinner. When I saw him, I automatically looked at the clock; it was seven thirty. The rest of the room was empty.

Does this work? I asked Erminia, pointing to the telephone mounted on the wall, next to the drink shelf.

Erminia nodded and handed me the glass with a smile. I walked over to the bar, tipped the cognac down my throat and, searching my pockets for coins, asked her to refill the glass. When Erminia complied with my request, I took the glass to the end of the bar, picked up the telephone, slid three hundred-peseta coins into the slot and dialed my mother's number.

Though she doesn't like to admit it, and in fact still officially resides in Barcelona in the same apartment that I live in, the truth is that for more than six years she's lived in Madrid with my sister and her husband, a French reporter working as a foreign correspondent for a Franco-German radio station. I hadn't seen her in six months, though I'd spoken to her on the phone a few

days earlier. Since she's usually the one who calls, she was alarmed
to hear my voice and thought something terrible had happened.

One always faces the past alone. It's possible to reach a certain
agreement about shared experiences, about the importance of
this or that event, but what's really interesting, what makes our
relationship to the past specific, a past which is nothing more
than the world of sensations whose memory continues to stir
inside us, is something personal and nontransferable, something
which has no way of being shared. Of course my mother was glad
and interested to hear that I had passed through Sant Honorat
for work and taken the opportunity to stop by our old house. But
after talking to her for a bit it occurred to me that I would never
really know what my mother felt looking back on those years,
and that, no matter how much I wanted to, I'd never succeed in
describing what I experienced when I revisited the place. Even so,
I didn't want to give up and, grasping at a straw, I told her about
the milk jug, yes, that tin jug we used to get milk from the farm
next door, that odd little jug with the funny lid, like a Tyrolean
hat. "No, dear, I can't say I remember that jug in particular," my
mother said, "but I do remember we'd go get milk from the farm
next door . . . What was the name of that farm?"

"Can Suni, Mom, it was called Can Suni," I told her, just as I
realized we were both alone, separated by places and experiences
that we nevertheless shared.

After I hung up I took a seat at the bar. Erminia was washing
dishes and once in a while lifted her head and looked at me out
of the corner of her eye, probably curious about the dejected look
on my face. I lit a cigarette. The blond man eating dinner behind
me asked, with an English accent, for a little more bread. His
words reached me wreathed in an exhalation of sadness.

"Have you any more bread?" the Englishman asked Erminia,
and this apparently harmless question only confirmed what I'd
sensed from my conversation with my mother. What was Sant
Honorat for this foreigner? A place he was passing through?

A business appointment? A name written on a planner? The place where he ate a heavy stew at seven thirty in the evening? Sant Honorat de Valldonzella: a name that suddenly became malleable, polysemous, labyrinthine. The Englishman's timely words stripped Sant Honorat of all the power I had granted it, at once removed all the mythical resonances this place held for me. The place I wanted to return to existed only inside me, had no foundation but my own memory. And the loneliness I now felt, the impossibility of making feelings collective, suddenly laid bare how frail the past is, how capricious the mind and how hollow its memories. And once again I felt myself being dragged toward the present, a present in which I existed only as a ghost, a hostile, unfamiliar present that had no room for any one of the impressions awakened inside me by the sight of an old milk jug, an old milk jug my mom couldn't even remember.

I knew then that my trip had come to an end. And that I would return empty-handed. In my past I wanted to unearth some semblance of coherence, some indication of a strength that could help me face the future, but now I felt even more lost and alone than when I'd arrived five days earlier. The boy I had been could offer me nothing more than a heap of useless memories, every bit as useless as if they belonged to someone else. Time had swept everything away, no bridge remained standing to take me back.

For a while I sat paralyzed, not knowing what to do. The memory of Barcelona loomed again. And I thought of Elisenda, too, and I told myself I should never have let our relationship end. I needed to keep drinking. I ordered another cognac and paid with a thousand-peseta bill. With the change I called my house. The answering machine picked up, and I entered my access code. I had two new messages. I listened to the first one: it was from Joaquín Huertas, a fellow lawyer with whom I'd signed up to go swimming twice a week at Piscinas Rasurell. He reminded me we'd signed up a month earlier and hadn't made it to the pool even once. He made a bad joke about paunches and cellulitis that I didn't hear the end of, because I pressed the button to delete the message. The voice on the answering machine told me that the second message had been left at 7:16 p.m. of that very day. I instinctively checked my watch. That was barely a half-hour ago. "Elisenda gets out of English class at six thirty," I thought. "This is the one I've been waiting for." For a moment I believed all was not lost, that I had a second chance. And as I began to imagine her back in the living room at her parents' house, this time wearing jeans and a black cotton T-shirt, quickly dialing the number to my house, I heard the beep that preceded the message, and then a man's voice belonging to one José Luis Marasco, secretary of the Department of Professional Ethics at the Bar Association, who very courteously made known his desire to meet with me and offered me his phone number so that I could get in touch with him at my earliest convenience; then he said good-bye and wished me a good evening.

I hung up the phone. I downed the cognac in one gulp . . . and asked Erminia to refill my glass.

I considered suicide. Then I decided to flee the country. A minute later I realized with irritation that I'd return to Barcelona that very night.

I asked Erminia where Ernest was, and she replied that he'd stepped out to buy some things at the supermarket but would be right back.

I tried to calm down, to think coolly. I couldn't. I grabbed the copy of that day's *La Vanguardia*, which lay on the bar under *El Mundo Deportivo* and *Sport*, and I began to flip through the pages. I felt indifferent to everything, no news could move me, I didn't care one bit about what was happening in the world. Maybe I had always been that way, maybe I never felt anything when I read that kind of news, and only now was depressed enough to admit it. Terrorist violence in Spain, floods in China, epidemics in Africa, massacres in the United States . . . What was I supposed to feel when I read all that? I moved directly to the entertainment section. I was no longer reading headlines, only paying attention to the photos of actresses, rock singers, bullfighters . . . Suddenly, as I turned the page, my eye stopped on a small photo on the right. The man in the photograph, with a sizable cigarette hanging from his lips, looked familiar, but

I couldn't quite place him. I read the caption: "Óscar Music, author and director of the play." My eyes then looked for the headline: "Opening Today: *Sweat*, a Bittersweet Comedy about Housewives." I glanced through the article before starting to read it and caught two adjectives: "luminous" and "deft." Then I decided to stop reading and put the newspaper back where I'd found it.

Ernest arrived a few minutes later. He walked into the restaurant with three or four bags from Caprabo in each hand. I got up to help him but he quickly stopped me.

"Don't get up," he commanded, gesturing to my barstool with his minuscule chin. "This is my job. Please don't trouble yourself on my account."

"As a matter of fact, I was looking for you," I said, sitting back down. "I wanted to ask you to total my bill. I have to leave tonight."

"What do you mean? You're leaving us?" he exclaimed in surprise, as if the possibility that I would leave the hotel had at no time occurred to him. "I hope it's nothing serious."

"No, just something at work. I planned to stay a few more days, but in the end . . ."

"Well, we'll miss you very much," he said, and stood looking up at the ceiling with a thoughtful air.

I remembered I had one more cognac to pay for and asked Erminia how much I owed her.

"Don't worry about that, it's on the house," Ernest intervened. "It's *on the house*," he repeated, stressing every syllable.

It took me ten minutes to gather my things in the room. When I came back down to the lobby, Ernest was standing by the entrance, taping a paper sign to the door.

I set my bag down by the counter and walked over to read the sign. "Help Wanted: Reception Assistant," it said.

"There," he said, rubbing his hands together. "Sooner or later someone will bite, I think."

"Don't you think you'd have better luck if you taped it the other way around, so that it's visible from the street?" I ventured to ask.

Ernest thought for a few seconds.

"What an idiot I am sometimes!" he cried out, slapping his forehead with the heel of his palm. "You're right, of course. Anyway," he went on, with a shrug of indifference, "I'll fix it later. Let's get you taken care of. You must be in a hurry."

When he went behind the counter I handed him the keys to my room. He sighed, looking at me intently.

"You don't know how sad we are that you're leaving us."

"Me too, I've had a nice few days here," I said, handing him my Visa card.

Ernest was acting strange, with more self-confidence than he had shown over the preceding days. When he spoke, he no longer looked down at the floor or up at the ceiling, but fixed his enormous brown eyes on my face. After settling the bill, I went to shake his hand to say good-bye, but he came out from behind the counter, stepped forward with a smile and gave me a brief but vigorous hug. I could see the tip of the enormous birthmark under his shirt collar.

Before I opened the door, now with my back to the lobby, I heard Ernest's voice saying one more good-bye, and with shock I heard him say my name, my real name, not the false name I gave the day I arrived so that he wouldn't recognize me. I stopped in my tracks, turned around and saw Ernest smiling at me with an exaggerated wink, further distorting his already unfortunate features. Ashamed, short of breath, I murmured a timid good-bye and left the hotel.

Ernest's final farewell, that last ghastly expression, his right eye closed as if his eyelids had been stapled shut, his mouth contorted in an attempt to form a smile, would stay with me for the whole trip back to Barcelona.

He'd found me out. The bastard had found me out. He knew who I was, he probably knew from the first day. And nevertheless he said nothing until now. Probably so as not to put me in an awkward position. He didn't bear a grudge. He hadn't taken revenge for all those tricks my friends and I played on him as children. On the contrary: he treated me well, even better than the other guests. And at the last minute he couldn't resist, he had to show me that he knew who I was, that he recognized me, that he remembered me. As though he didn't mind that I had deceived him, as if the excitement of reconnecting with someone from the past meant more to him than the insult and slight (one more slight, poor Ernest) that my lie contained.

The town fool had managed to humiliate me. Not on purpose, but he had. And the humiliation and feelings of guilt were such that I no longer even thought about what was waiting for me (and wasn't waiting for me) back in Barcelona; I didn't think about Elisenda, or Señora Ruscarons, or José Luis Marasco, or perhaps I did think about all of them and for that very reason tried to focus my attention on a face, on a horrendous grimace full of humanity that combined all the anguish of my dark future.

When I got to the tollbooth at Mollet, I took out my Visa card and stuck it into the automated pay machine. When the green light came on and the barrier went up, I reached out to remove the card, but just then a sudden start paralyzed my body for a moment. The vehicle behind me honked its horn. I grabbed my card and, as if I still had any doubts about the name embossed on it, I switched on the light inside the car and read slowly: Carlos Mestres Ruiz. (That's my name.) And I realized how foolish I had been.

In all likelihood, Ernest had only realized I'd used a false name when he looked at the card I handed him to pay the hotel bill. Even then he hadn't associated me with that brat from Barcelona who teased him as a child. Now that I thought about it (how difficult thinking can be sometimes, and how easy it is once you start thinking straight and everything makes sense and falls into place!), Ernest wouldn't have known my last name. No one in town called me by my last name when we were children, and my first name is too common for him to put two and two together and recognize me. No, he didn't recognize me. And that made my deceit something insignificant, pointless. Ernest probably even found it exciting and fun to have a guest who concealed his real identity. He couldn't resist giving me a knowing wink: "You must have your reasons for going around with a false name," the poor guy probably thought.

I breathed a sigh of relief. The car behind me honked for the fourth time. I put the Visa in my glove compartment, turned off the light inside the car, stuck my hand out the window in a closed fist and, in an unusual gesture for me, raised my middle finger to offer it to the driver behind me. Then I sped off.

10

IN THE BATHROOM, facing the mirror. Four thirty in the morning. The fluorescent bulb's dirty, violent light forces me to close my eyes. When I reopen them I can't quite make out who's standing before me. I know the face, of course: those irregular features, that flat nose, those dark, overly round eyes, those lips hanging open as you gape back at me . . . I recognize what I see, but I feel like I don't know who the face belongs to, like it doesn't belong to anyone, like there's nothing at all inside that sickly pale skin, those dark, overly round eyes. Who's in there? With effort I can make out a flicker of life, the remains of a will, the hint of something trying to be something I recognize . . . but that flicker quickly vanishes, and blankness returns to those eyes that are no longer looking at me but seem stuck halfway between the mirror and my face. You're not listening. You don't want to listen. Are you really me? And what does it mean to be me? Where do I end and you begin? You look so strange, so foreign . . . and yet we're joined by an indissoluble bond, there's no denying that. I notice my arms swinging uncontrollably, seeming to blow in a wind that isn't there. And then I pretend to get indignant and demand answers. You've got to take responsibility, I shout, and I stand there looking at him, waiting for a response. And now my entire figure is swaying, rocking back and forth. You shouldn't drink like that. It's really not good for you. It's not good for either of us. You have a body and need to be able to keep it all under control. That's what you're supposed to be here for, that's why I carry you around. I'm a point at the intersection of every worry, every anxiety, every fear in the world. Adrift. And you're not doing a thing. Someone should seize control, grab the helm, rebuild, rebuild, rebuild, reeee-bbbuild. I can't tell anymore if you're indifferent or if you really can't hear me. Dereliction of duty, dereliction of duty, dereliction of duty. With that stupid grin on your face . . .

All morning it poured. In the afternoon, when I went outside, I learned that some outlying neighborhoods had even been flooded. "The damage is incalculable," I overheard one passerby say to another. The rain must have really come down, since the noise woke me up. But not before noon. The hangover was brutal. Hundreds of burning needles jabbed me in the head, drawn by the thread of a clumsy and exceedingly slow seamstress. Sudden, violent jerks, occurring at variable intervals, made me see stars, the big dipper in extreme close-up.

Once again, my good intentions would have to wait. I planned to go to the office that morning to talk to Santasusana about the message that Marasco, from the Bar Association, had left me. He may well have known about it, since a few years back Santasusana was on the board of directors. If so, I could rest assured that he'd offer to intervene in the matter. But obviously I was in no state for such niceties. Besides, I still had time: it was Friday and no one was expecting me back at the office until Monday, and I was in no rush to get in touch with Marasco.

A thick nebula obscured the previous night. I had trouble falling asleep, that much I remembered. It had been rough coming back to the mess, the silence, with Elisenda's absence still imprinted on every object, on every wall, running through every inch of the apartment. I couldn't find any sleeping pills (Elisenda must have taken the packet of Vincosedan I kept by my razor), so I took a drink straight from a bottle of Anís del Mono, convinced that a couple of swigs would be enough to knock me out. Of what happened next I remembered very little. The bottle now stood empty on my desk next to a compendium of provincial law.

The day didn't inspire me to get out of bed, but my bladder was about to burst, so I gathered my courage, put my feet on the floor, and ran to the bathroom. The amount of liquid I expelled would have refilled the bottle of Anís del Mono and then some. (Occasionally one's mind can't help but linger on such musings.) Afterward, I was about to wash my face when I saw, as I turned on the faucet, that the mirror was cracked. A fracture ran lengthwise up the mirror, and from it spread dozens of very fine lines like the tributaries of a river on a map. Down from the center of the crack trickled a teardrop of dried blood (oh, it was all so cinematic!). Then I looked at my hands. On my right hand, stuck to my knuckles, I discovered a grainy pulp that I immediately identified as a mixture of blood and toilet paper. I began to remember.

I cleaned the wound with soap and water and replaced the toilet paper with an inconspicuous Band-Aid. I got back in bed.

The Bloody Mary was starting to fill up with the typical Friday night crowd: young people downing their last drinks before storming the discos (where a mixed drink can be prohibitively expensive), along with one or two regulars at the bar putting off going home. Alberto had spent over an hour inserting coins into the slot machine. I watched from a barstool, leaning against the wooden bar.

"How much have you spent?" I asked for the fourth time, by then without the least hope of getting a response. "Seven thousand? Eight thousand? Don't you think that's a ridiculous waste of money?"

Alberto pounded the buttons without conviction, with a suspicious calm, but he didn't take his eyes off the machine, not even when he brought the pint of beer up to his lips. Every ten or fifteen minutes, the time it took him to polish off two thousand pesetas, he'd reach for his wallet and take out another bill, which he'd hand to me to get change from the bartender.

"Are we going be here much longer? Like I said, I haven't eaten a thing in twenty-four hours. I'd like to eventually get dinner, if we could."

"Just a minute, I'm almost finished," mumbled Alberto at last.

"Almost finished with what?" I insisted. "Your money? You sound like you're on a mission, like you're required to stick coins in that machine. For what? Setting aside the fact that you're not going to win anything, what would happen if you did hit the jackpot? What would that change? I just don't see the point. You don't need the money . . ."

Before I finished speaking I realized how ill-advised my comment was.

"I mean . . ." I tried to backpedal, but it was already too late. Alberto lost interest in the machine and turned toward me, pointing at me with his beer.

"You really want to know what I get out of these machines? Do you want to know why I'm capable of burning through not just six or seven thousand pesetas, as you so naively suppose, but twelve or thirteen, or even twenty thousand, if necessary? Do you want to know why?" He set down his beer on the bar and pulled up a barstool. "It's because I'm sick of everything, sick of this world, of other people, of my life, sick and tired of everything, e-ve-ry-thing. If I could I would do nothing else. Twenty-four hours plugged into a slot machine: that's my dream. To replace this shitty world with the electronic circuitry of this device. You should try it. You pull here and set the universe in motion. A simple, straightforward universe, with fixed rules. And you lose: of course you lose, you always lose. That's the point. To play to lose, to give yourself over to defeat, to fulfill your destiny in a perfect, known, comprehensible microcosm free of lies and deception. Once in a while you line up three in a row, and that's when the miracle occurs: a mirage of unity, of harmony, as if time shrunk to a single point and gathered within it the whole pathetic mystery of this whole goddamned life. And those few seconds, as ridiculous as it sounds to you, are the only good thing I have left these days. Money? Money has nothing to do with this." He sat down on the stool and lit a cigarette; I rather sheepishly avoided looking at him directly in the face. "In any case," he went on, lowering his voice slightly, "since I can see it's a subject you're obsessed with, you should know that you're misinformed. Things have changed: we're not millionaires anymore. The Cisnerrososes are ruined, debts are eating up the family fortune. It's over, kaput, gone to seed. The only consolation I have left is that I wasn't the one who caused the calamity. For once I'm not to blame."

"What do you mean? What happened?" I asked, as confused as if I'd just been told of a sudden death. "That's impossible. Are you sure?"

"It was my brother, the family genius. He came back from the U.S. waving his MBA in the air. No one dared question him, even though it was clear from day one that what he was proposing was financial suicide. He recommended we buy a bankrupt company, a company which made automotive accessories and which would, he said, be turning a handsome profit again within two years. After just a few months we had to triple the initial investment. And by then it was too late to back out. Up until the last minute my dad trusted my brother, but things didn't work. Market saturation. Anyway, you get the picture. The point is, now we're in the bank's hands. Any day now they'll seize the house in the south of France."

"Wow, I didn't know. I'm really sorry," I said, sticking to formulas of condolence. "But it can't be all that bad . . . and besides, didn't you have your own money? The inheritance from your grandfather . . ."

"My grandfather's inheritance is scattered among the bars of this city. There's hardly any left. Money is for spending, after all. Besides, it was less than you think. People say a lot of things."

We finished our beers in silence, watching the tables full of younger patrons getting louder and drunker. Then Alberto got up from the stool and gave me a pat on the back.

"Let's eat, you must be starving," he said, shaking out his overcoat. "Oh, and dinner's on me, I can still afford it."

We picked up the conversation again an hour later, sitting in front of a steak tartare and a bottle of El Coto red.

"With or without money, my life's not worth a cent. I'm thirty-four years old and I haven't accomplished a thing. And at this point I'm not going to. I'm useless. Don't get me wrong, I have no regrets. People are who they are. I hate making plans,

I don't like to map out my life, to put it to some instrumental use with the future in mind. I can't, it depresses me. The very idea of starting a family, setting reasonable goals, nurturing little ambitions, makes me sick. And anyway, it's not like I know how to do anything, so even if I wanted to . . ."

"What about literature? Do you still write?"

"Do I still write? Please, Carlos, don't make me laugh. I never actually wrote anything. Literature isn't for me. It was an excuse, a false alibi so people would think I was doing something and leave me alone. I would have liked to write, it's true, and for a while I tried, I swear I tried, but I knew from the start there was no use."

"Maybe you gave up too soon. I mean, I imagine it takes patience. You've read a lot, and you're creative, and you're really smart . . . Look at your friend Óscar Music. If someone like him can do it . . ."

"Ah, Carlos, such a kidder. Sometimes you seem like you were raised in the jungle by a family of monkeys. The two things have nothing to do with each other. I'm creative? Smart? Who knows, maybe I am. But explain to me how you turn that into literature. Óscar is a knuckle-dragging boor, it's true, but somehow he sits down to write and does it well. Whereas I sit down to write and I'm like a seven-year-old. And another thing: I haven't read half the writers I talk about. It's all a lie, just one more way to amuse myself. Deep down reading bores me, it's always bored me. On the other hand, I do love discussing literature, especially if I have no clue what I'm talking about. If people buy it, that's not my problem."

I made as if to start to speak, but he cut me off abruptly.

"Never mind, it doesn't matter. And anyway, that's not what I'm talking about. I've already said I have no ambitions, there's nothing I aspire to be and nothing I aspire to do. I'm glad I'm not of these guys." He motioned with his head to indicate everyone around him. "The problem is, I've lost interest in life. For a long time all I needed was excess: to burn every moment, to have women, alcohol, the night . . . But something's changed. I guess we're getting older, Carlitos. Some things are only for the young."

"Well, to judge by the life you lead, you'd hardly know it."

"It's true, I still drink, I still go out at night, I still hold on to every instant with an endearing fervor, I even hook up from time to time . . . But all those things used to make me happy, and were a reason for joy, and now they're just a mode of survival. I don't know how else to live. And it's getting harder and harder to see the point."

Something in Alberto's words, in his tone, in the gesticulations that punctuated his speech, revealed an absolute despair, a profound and unrelenting weariness. It seemed useless to say anything. In fact, I was convinced that even though he was addressing me, Alberto was talking to himself, as though he needed to verbalize his disappointment but didn't care whether or not anyone was listening. And once again I felt that same solitude, that terrible powerlessness I felt a few days earlier when I realized, as I told Alberto my troubles, that no matter how willing he was to listen to me, he'd never really know the true measure of my suffering. The same thing was happening now. Alberto was far away. His words gave me only a general picture—too vague, too imprecise—of what he was going through. And then, as I kept listening, I understood that friendship, like love, is just a game of appearances, an amusement which might make existence more bearable, but which at no point, despite often making us think otherwise, ever quite saves us from our loneliness and isolation.

Alberto was Alberto, I was me. And even if this conclusion was obvious and natural and inescapable, it didn't for all that seem any less cruel or devastating.

After dinner we lost ourselves in Barcelona. Once again we drank too much. We ended up at seven in the morning singing the Hare Krishna in front of the cathedral. We must not have been too bad, because a German tourist tossed us a hundred-peseta coin and asked to have her picture taken with us.

11

MONDAY CAME. BACK to the office. I spent Saturday and Sunday relaxing. My alcoholism was beginning to take on worrying proportions, so in anticipation of the week ahead, I had forbidden Alberto to tempt me again with new nighttime excursions.

At nine o'clock sharp I stepped through the office doors. Luisa told me that Santasusana had just arrived. I decided to go straight to his office.

Santasusana was on his feet, talking on the phone. He motioned to me to take a seat. "Be right with you," he said, covering the receiver with his hand. He was speaking heatedly and gesticulating a great deal. I had rarely seen him like this, raising his voice more than strictly necessary, picking his free ear with his pinky finger, stomping his foot every time the person on the other end said something objectionable. I couldn't piece together what was the matter, but it must have been important. I thought I heard him say something about his daughter, and he repeatedly mentioned a lack of professionalism, unacceptable risks, a scam, embassies . . . "I'm going to call the Spanish embassy right now," he said. And he threatened to sue someone. "If this isn't straightened out within two hours, there will be hell to pay!" he roared. As for me, I began to see that this wasn't the best time to talk about my problems. But it would look bad if I suddenly got up and left his office with no explanation. If only I could light a cigarette!

After Santasusana hung up, he stood looking out the window silently for a moment. Then, as though suddenly remembering my presence, he turned around and shook my hand.

"Sorry for keeping you waiting, but I'm very busy."

"Everything all right?" I asked with curiosity.

"No, but it's nothing serious, I hope. It's my daughter. Last week she left to spend a few weeks in England. One of those exchange programs, you know the type. The poor girl wanted to learn English. Well, yesterday she calls me up, bawling, and tells me her host parents went out of town for a few days and left her in charge of their three children. Can you imagine the scene? The youngest isn't even one year old! They won't stop crying, of course, and my poor Sandra, who hasn't changed a diaper in her life, doesn't know what to do and, understandably, is at her wits' end. The people at the program say they're trying to locate the parents. But they're lying through their teeth! How can they find them if they left no address, no phone number, nothing at all? I told them they need to send someone to the house to take care of the kids until the parents get back, but they say they have no one available in the area. Can you believe it? And my Sandra's not even sixteen!"

"Goodness, that's awful."

"But this isn't over yet. Don't worry, this isn't over."

He picked up the phone and told his secretary to get him the number of the Spanish embassy in London.

"Anyway, how are you? Were you able to rest?" he asked, setting down the receiver.

"I was. I think taking a few days off did me some good."

"Wonderful," he said, then winked. "So now back to work, I assume?"

"Yes, of course. The . . . How should I . . . Regarding the matter of Señora Ruscarons, the other day I got a message from the Bar Association . . . but I suppose now's not the time."

"Oh, right. They called here. I think Luisa gave them your home number. Have you spoken to them yet?"

"No, not yet . . . In fact, I thought that perhaps . . ."

Luisa walked into the office just then with the number for the Spanish embassy on a small piece of paper.

"Thanks, Luisa," said Santasusana, taking the piece of paper in his hand. And then he turned to me: "Talk to them. The sooner you get this matter settled, the better. Let me know how it goes," he added, raising his eyebrows and picking up the telephone again.

I stayed a few seconds longer in Santasusana's office, but seeing how nervously he dialed the phone, I saw that I shouldn't take up any more of his time.

I left with a slight wave good-bye, even though he was no longer looking at me. Somewhere in England someone had answered a phone.

"*Good morning?* What do you mean, *good morning?* Isn't this the goddamn Spanish embassy?"

Really, I had never seen him so worked up.

I spent the rest of the morning drafting some lawsuits I hadn't finished and talking to Maserachs about the cases we'd received during my weeklong absence. At lunchtime I called Marasco. I'd written down his cell phone number on the stationery Elisenda forgot to take with her (or maybe she left it for me as a keepsake?). The call was short, almost telegraphic. "Can you swing by my office at the Bar Association this afternoon or evening? I'll be there until nine, at least."

"Sure, sounds good."

"See you this evening, then." And then he hung up. I probably caught him at a bad time, too. In any case, his casual tone was a good sign. He considered me a colleague. We were in the same boat. God bless professional solidarity!

You resist your fate and all you do is hasten things along, draw events closer, ensure the inevitable. Ignoring the obvious, you start to accumulate symptoms and conditions and ailments that sooner or later impose their law, like an overinflated balloon that finally bursts to free itself of the excess air. Maybe it's better that way. Perhaps cowards like us, unable to avert a crisis, inclined to indefinitely postpone the right decision, know that the only way we can change things is to let reality reach its logical extreme, its final limit, because then there's no more choice and nothing to lose, nothing to do but cut the ties and start over from scratch, this time without all the baggage accumulated over the years.

Unable to face my professional failure, my limits, my lack of interest in the law, I surrendered to an inertia that could lead me only to disaster.

At first it had all been very nice: the thrill of achieving the social status that comes with being a lawyer, the rush of finding the right words to drive home a brilliant point in a trial and garner murmurs of approval in the courtroom, the satisfaction of appearing before clients as a powerful protector, the coquettishness of sharing a professional jargon with colleagues, the sense of being at home in the courthouse or the offices of the Bar Association, the pride of earning those first professional fees, the prospects of success, the narcissistic pleasure of giving free advice to family and friends: the profession's glitter and allure, which nevertheless quickly fade.

Too soon responsibilities and routines began to outweigh the benefits and small pleasures that practicing law afforded me. The enthusiasm of the first few months gave way to apathy and boredom. And then came the doubts. And I started to wonder whether I hadn't made a mistake, whether I was any good at the job. More and more I dreaded trials, and I had a hard time keeping up with Maserachs. I knew I'd never be a good lawyer and was doomed to mediocrity. But it was too late to turn back—or that's what I told myself in order to put off making a decision, to put off facing reality just yet. And then came the excuses and the evasive demurrals, and little by little I began to take refuge in increasingly harmless, routine tasks. And I didn't feel all bad. After all, I was still a lawyer. There's nothing wrong with being a lawyer. Being a lawyer is nothing to sneeze at. In this way I persisted in the delusion.

But when decisions are delayed, the situation deteriorates. And there comes a time when any incident provides an excuse for fate to impose itself; the smallest trouble, the slightest departure from routine, ends up taking on monumental proportions and becoming a real threat. You miss a hearing and the world falls on top of you, you feel you've committed the gravest of sins and the entire population is out in the streets ready to string you up. And you continue to cling to the delusion. "I'm still a lawyer, I can still fight back," you tell yourself. But you have neither the strength nor the courage. Then come a few more missteps, and soon you're taking swings in the dark. Events get the better of you. And suddenly one day reality bars your way. You've reached the end of the line.

At seven thirty that evening I waited outside the offices of the Bar Association. I circled the block twice, walked past the entrance several times without going in. I was nervous, too nervous. And I felt uncomfortable in my body. I still felt the aftereffects of my last bender: the alcoholic's inability to ignore his own expressions when sober. It's as if a mirror in front of my eyes registered the slightest movement of my facial muscles. There was only one solution: to have a couple of drinks to get back to normal.

I sat down at the counter of a small establishment across the street from the Bar Association headquarters and ordered a gin and tonic. I downed it in a few gulps. Since I was the only customer, there was a strong chance I'd have to fend off the bartender's onslaught. And sure enough, as he served me my second gin and tonic, he began to talk to me about football. "I'm a Madrid fan," I said, aloof, assuming that such a statement would settle the matter and keep him away for a good while. But I was wrong. The bartender's face lit up. "I'm a Madrid fan, too!" he shouted in delight. That poor man must have waited for years for one of his fellow fans to walk into that bar. He produced some peanuts and almonds, which I didn't pretend to be excited about. Then he said we had to celebrate the most recent Cup (which Cup was he talking about? I've never seen a match the whole way through!), and he took a bottle of peach liqueur and two chilled shot glasses from the refrigerator. We drank to Real Madrid, then to the Cibeles Fountain; I made the third toast at the bartender's insistence ("Come on, come on, now it's your turn"): "To Di Stefano!" I shouted, hesitating (did Di Stefano play for Real Madrid? I didn't have it all together). "To Di Stefano!" he shouted, removing all doubt. I let him go on. I simply nodded once in a while. He responded by refilling my glass every time it was empty. When I was on the seventh shot, the tables in the bar began to levitate. The bartender's voice reached my ears like a distant hum. It must have been past nine. I stood up with difficulty, trying to prop myself up on the bar. "I have to go now, I've got something to do," I said, stumbling to the exit. Even now I shudder to imagine the poor bartender's face when he saw me leave in that state, without so much as thanking him for the shots.

Once outside, to try to minimize the swaying in my steps, I fixed my eyes on the entrance to the Bar Association offices and began to walk toward it. But I concentrated so intently on that bright rectangle abuzz with men in ties coming and going that I didn't realize I was crossing a street, Calle de Mallorca, where vehicular traffic is not unusual. I recalled the existence of said street upon hearing the drawn-out, plaintive screech of a car slamming on the brakes. I then turned to my right to see a Ford Escort barreling down on me. With no time to get out of the way, I closed my eyes and leapt up with all my might to avoid getting pinned under the wheels. I landed on the hood of the car, which deflected the blow and threw me onto the ground. I lay sprawled on the asphalt.

A crowd quickly gathered around me. Everyone was asking the same thing: was I all right, could I move, should they call an ambulance. Strangely enough, no one gave me their business card, though it must have occurred to more than one of them. "It's nothing, I'm fine," I reassured them. The driver of the Ford Escort, an older woman who looked like Margaret Thatcher, apologized profusely and held her head in her trembling hands. "Please, ma'am, calm down. I'm fine, really," I said with commendable aplomb. It's odd, neither the impact nor the preceding fright diminished my drunkenness, but instead magnified it. I felt euphoric. I couldn't remember ever having caused such a commotion. When I began to slowly pick myself up, I thought

I heard a familiar voice—an unpleasant, nasal voice. I looked up and there was Maserachs, offering me his hand. This wasn't surprising: Ricardo was jockeying for a position as professor of labor law at the postgraduate School of Legal Practice and spent all day at the Bar Association offices trying to find someone to kiss up to. "Are you sure you're all right, Carlos? Sure you're not hurt?" Once people saw that Maserachs knew me and was taking care of me, they started to leave.

"Yes, I'm fine. Get your hands off me, I can manage by myself."

"All right, then. I'll give you a lift home".

"No way, I'm not going home. I have an appointment with Marasco and I don't intend to miss it. I'm going to tell that ass-hole where to stick it."

Luckily, Maserachs saw what state I was in. "You reek of booze, my friend," he said in disgust, "you reek of booze." I insisted I wanted to go to my appointment, but then Maserachs became very serious: didn't I realize what I was doing, what was wrong with me, didn't I see I couldn't even talk straight, everyone could tell I was drunk, why couldn't I find somewhere else to put on such a sorry scene, I was going to sully Santasusana's good name, he wasn't about to let a brat like me ruin so many years' hard work, I was pathetic, I was selfish, and on and on and on.

And listening to Maserachs, as the drunkenness began to wear off, I suddenly realized that something important had just happened to my life: the spectacle I just made of myself had pushed me over the edge and left me suspended in midair, where bridges can't be rebuilt and the final drop is only a matter of time. I realized, in short, that my career as a lawyer was over.

12

AFTER PARKING IN front of my building, Maserachs took out a pack of Marlboros and offered one to me. We smoked in silence for a few minutes. I felt uncomfortable. I was about to ask if I could go, but I sensed Ricardo was preparing a speech and didn't want to interrupt. I owed him one, after all. "Listen, you've got to reassess your priorities, you can't go on like this," went the beginning of his sermon. The litany that followed was entirely predictable, and after a few moments I stopped listening. I pretended to listen, of course, and nodded steadily, but my mind was already somewhere else, slipping into that other life that was beginning to take shape on the horizon. We sat in the car for over half an hour, at which point Maserachs stopped speaking and placed both hands on the wheel of his minivan. I realized he had finished. I could leave. We said good-bye with a handshake (people get so solemn when offering advice!), and I got out and headed toward the front door of my building. Ricardo Maserachs started the engine and rolled down his window. "Think about what I said," he advised. I nodded again, and he stepped on the gas.

I had my keys in hand and was about to open the door, but when I heard him drive off, I decided to put the keys back in my pocket and walk down the street.

I felt like walking. I wanted to drift through the streets and feel the night wind, cool on my face. I wanted to give mobility to my thoughts, to contrast them with the anarchic rhythm of my steps, to stride undramatically, unheroically into the inevitable transformation which from that moment onward would radically alter my life. I wanted, above all, to lose myself in the crowd, become one of those tiny dots, those hundreds of dots indistinguishable from one another that you can make out from the sky as you circle the city in an airplane, dots you try to follow with your eyes, and sometimes even pick out at random and ask: who is that one? Where is he going? Is he a good person? What regrets does he carry with him? How many dreams? Is he in love? Is there someone else, another minuscule dot, thinking of him at this very moment? How long does he have until he dies? Is his body perhaps already harboring a cancer that his mind is oblivious to? Is he happy? What does he do? Who did he vote for in the last elections? Is he a winner? Is he anxious about the future? From up there the possible answers are so insignificant, and everything looks so small, so trivial and pointless and inconsequential, that for a few seconds you get the impression that life is nothing but a game we've taken too seriously. Perhaps now, as I walked down Balmes toward the Ramblas, someone looking out the window of an airplane was following me with their eyes, too, and thinking about the marvelous triviality of my existence. Of course, now that I thought about it, since it was dark out, they would have a hard time seeing me from so high up.

When I reached Plaza de Cataluña, after walking for an hour, I took comfort in seeing that, even though it was ten minutes after midnight on a Monday night, a lot of people were still out on the Ramblas. All kinds of people were there: couples walking up to Plaza de Cataluña, where a cab would take them home, groups of youngsters heading to the bars in Plaza Real, cigarette sellers, hash dealers, prostitutes, three living statues waiting for a coin, a pair of cops, pickpockets lurking behind a kiosk on Calle del Hospital, tourists, buskers packing up their things . . . But I soon realized there was another group, people I had never noticed but who had nevertheless (now that I saw them I had no doubt) always been there. They were men (I didn't see any women) who had no set course and weren't there for any specific reason or purpose. They never stopped walking, less for the exercise than to make sure they weren't noticed. Only occasionally did they stop at some tavern and drink silently at the bar. And then they kept on walking. They were simply there, nothing more. They weren't heading home or to work or anywhere at all, and they weren't looking for fun. All they did was inhabit that street, that plot of earth in the depths of a city. They didn't do anything.

They weren't waiting for anything. There was no nervous look in their eyes, no boredom, no anxiety, no joy, no loneliness . . . They had no schedules or responsibilities, or at any rate, if they did, they had learned to behave as though they didn't. And that's why they went unnoticed. That's why I had never seen them. They were there that night and they would be there the next night. At some point they would disappear, go unobtrusively home, worn out by the exhaustion of doing nothing. And then they would return hours later, once night had fallen again. They blended into the background and no one paid them any attention. But I paid attention to them that night, and the more I watched them the more I felt convinced that part of me, a part I had persisted in ignoring until then, had somehow always been there, with them, doing nothing, waiting for nothing, merely occupying that street indefinitely.

And I thought about Alberto Cisnerroso, too, about what he had said a few days earlier. At the time I felt I didn't understand what he meant—or rather, I felt incapable of putting myself in his place or feeling what he felt: but now, all of a sudden, seized by an overpowering lucidity, I found that his words not only made sense, but seemed, like beacons in the night, to illuminate my newly inaugurated future. And then I saw clearly that our friendship was true and deep, and inevitable, too, for we were bound by a common destiny. Not by chance did I think to call him that afternoon, two weeks back, when the life I clung to, as I probably sensed but didn't fully realize, had begun to crumble.

Normal people come into this world in order to be someone, to accomplish some important or necessary task, to make something useful of their life, something worthy or productive. Sooner or later those people find their place in the world. And while the place they find is seldom, or almost never, the place they dreamed of, it hardly matters, because that's part of the game, and frustration only sparks their imagination and spurs them onward. This is how they pass their time.

Alberto wasn't one of those people, and neither, I now began

to realize, was I. We hadn't been invited to the game. We didn't
have a place set aside for us in the world. Alberto had known
from the beginning, and from the beginning had made his life
a preemptive, definitive act of giving up; I, on the other hand,
blind to my destiny, tried to join in the game and grab hold of a
life that wasn't mine, a normal life like millions of people lead, a
viable, desirable life that nevertheless didn't belong to me.

Alberto and I, like those denizens of the Ramblas whom I
now watched with tenderness and camaraderie, weren't cut out
for that life; being someone was not within our reach, we weren't
capable of accomplishing important or useful or productive tasks.
We were here and we were alive, certainly, but we inhabited the
world like mice living in a house whose owners tolerate them as
long as they don't stray from their hidden, subterranean routes.
I had strayed. I even believed I had found my place, that I was
someone, that I had a part to play in the normal order of things.
But I was lying to myself. And lying to everyone else. For a long
time I kept up the lie. And now it was all over—pathetically,
embarrassingly, which is how these things always end, which
is what always happens when you strive to achieve something
beyond your capabilities. And still, neither the pathos nor the
embarrassment of recent events could overshadow the enormous
pleasure and peace of mind I now felt, realizing I was right back
where I'd started. "My life, my real life, starts now," I thought to
myself. And I was amazed that this new life consisted of nothing,
that it held no goals for the future, no ambitions, no purpose,
nothing at all—only being adrift, like a leaf swept away by the
current of a river.

After walking for a long time, I ended up sitting on a bench on
the Paseo de Colón. I was beat. Too many emotions in a single
day. Besides, while at first I thought I had walked away from my
brush with the Ford Escort without a scratch, now a pain was
stirring in my right knee, a pain that wasn't too intense but grew
worse with every step. I lit a cigarette and decided to rest for a

good while. I'm not sure how it happened, but in spite of the roar of the passing cars on either side of the Paseo, I dozed off. And then my dreams, with their usual irritating, defiant insistence, lifted me through the night back to the headquarters of the Bar Association, and more specifically to Marasco's office, where I'd been expected that afternoon for an appointment which fortunately never took place. Now my canceled appointment would play out inside my head. More people sat in attendance than had originally been summoned. Of course the host was there, don José Luis Marasco, a middle-aged man with inscrutable features who punctuated every sentence with a cruel, demeaning smile, but so were Santasusana, and Señora Ruscarons, and Maserachs. Intimidated by the probing gaze of everyone present, I sunk back into the leather armchair and mumbled unintelligible rebuttals to the accusations leveled against me. At one point, tired of Marasco's sermons and Maserachs's fawning nods, and determined to put an end to all the humiliation, I climbed atop the desk and launched into a tap dance. Astonishingly, this display of flamenco panache found a warm welcome among the audience, and what until then had been long faces and dirty looks became smiles and cheering grins. Señora Ruscarons, moved by the spirit, didn't hesitate to let loose with an "olé" after my most impressive moves, and even Marasco began to clap his hands to the rhythm. But just then the door opened and in walked an older man wearing a judge's robe. He was rather heavyset and sported a well-trimmed silver beard. High on the enthusiasm of my audience, I didn't stop dancing, and even welcomed the newcomer with an expert turn and a flamenco shout. I quickly noticed, however, that the others had stopped watching me and now stood at attention facing the judge. "What is the meaning of this?" the judge demanded.

"It's Carlos Mestres Ruiz, Your Honor, I've spoken to you about him before," Marasco hastened to explain.

"Indeed . . . so this is Carlos Mestres Ruiz? Well, well, well. We meet at last. Excellent." I then stopped dancing and looked down at Santasusana from the tabletop, taken aback, pleading for an explanation. "And now he's come here to mock us, has he?" continued the judge, not taking his eyes off of me. "Very well. We'll see who has the last laugh," he said, and swinging his hips briskly, he shouted: "Quick, grab him, don't let him escape, the police are on their way." And all together, Maserachs, Marasco, Santasusana, and Ruscarons leapt at me and pulled me down off the table. Maserachs sat on my chest, knees pinning my arms. Marasco set to work immobilizing my legs. I looked to Santasusana for mercy, since after leaping at me he had fallen back.

"I'm sorry, there's nothing I can do," he said, not repressing a little smile. "The fact is, the judge is right: this time you've gone too far. But don't worry, at the police station all they'll do is stick a rat up your ass—you just have to ride it out." After saying this he began to roar with laughter. I understood less and less of what was happening and broke down. I cried uncontrollably and begged them to release me. But they all ignored my pleas. Señora Ruscarons, who seemed more than a little tipsy, had started making advances at the judge, moving her right leg slightly forward and slowly lifting her skirt. The judge stroked his chin and nodded with interest. Far away a police siren began to wail. I could see the veins in my neck bulging, turning blue. I was about to explode. But just at that moment I felt a tickling in my nose, and all of a sudden a powerful sneeze expelled the dream images from my head and brought me back to the reality of the Paseo de Colón.

"What a relief," I said, "what a relief—it was only a dream." But even though I had escaped from the nightmare, I didn't wholly regain my calm. A deep uneasiness lingered in my body. It was cold. In the sky the clouds began to part and the sea breeze pierced my skin and numbed my bones and joints. It's strange and uncomfortable to wake up in the middle of the street. Trucks went barreling by, heading toward Mercabarna. The city readied itself to receive a new day. To make matters worse, my hangover was back, and I didn't know whether to chalk up the trembling of my hands to the cold or the alcohol withdrawal.

I looked at my watch. It was a quarter to seven. If I hailed a cab, in less than twenty minutes I could be curled up in bed, feet toasty and sheets pulled up to my nose. But before I could go home I still had to do one thing. Yes, had to: now it felt like a duty, but a few hours earlier, before I fell asleep on the bench, I could hardly wait for the moment to arrive when I could go find Elisenda. Now I didn't feel like it. Too sluggish, too tired, too cold, too hungover. Nor were my thoughts as clear as they had been a few hours before. But I had to do it. I had to talk with Elisenda. "If I don't do it now, I'll never do it," I thought. I didn't feel up to it, but it was an existential imperative. I couldn't move on from my previous life until I had the chance to tell her my version of what had happened between us.

Very slowly, throwing all my weight on my left leg so as not to overburden my battered knee, I stood up and dug around in my pockets to see how much money I had. Nine hundred pesetas was all I found. If I saved four hundred for the cab, that still left five hundred to get two or three cans of beer. Just to be safe, I could also get money from an ATM, but from where I stood there were no banks in sight, and besides, I had to get used to spending less: I couldn't pretend that money wouldn't be one of the biggest challenges to overcome in my new life. So I decided to make do with what I had.

Alternately limping and hopping, I reached a bar at the bottom of the Ramblas whose door was half open. At first the owner said he was closed and told me to come back in ten minutes, but eventually, after some insistence, I got him to sell me the beer, and even to drop the price by ten pesetas, which was the amount I needed to get the third can. I also bummed a cigarette, since I had none left.

Once I'd solved my alcohol supply problem, I went to look for a cab. I took out a can from the plastic bag and began to drink. I looked at my watch again: it was five to seven. Elisenda started work at the Hospital Clínico at 8:00 a.m. Considering her parents lived two blocks from the hospital, I figured that, if I wanted to find her, I should reach her parents' house by a quarter to eight. In theory I had plenty of time. But I began to worry when two empty cabs came by, one after the other, and ignored my obvious waving and kept on driving. It then occurred to me that perhaps I didn't look especially presentable, and that if I were a cab driver, I might not have risked picking up someone drinking beer at seven in the morning with hair and clothes that looked like mine. I decided to down the first can, tuck in my shirt, and comb my hair a bit with my hands. And a few minutes later another free cab came by, and my efforts were rewarded.

"I'm going to Córcega and Villarroel," I told the driver, "but I might have to get out sooner, I'll let you know." At that time of day traffic in Barcelona moved fairly briskly, but even so my budget of four hundred pesetas looked like it might come up short. I spent the whole trip clenching my buttocks and crossing my fingers, convinced, I'm not sure why, that doing so would somehow slow down the fare meter. As we drove along Mallorca, just before the intersection with Casanova, it reached four hundred pesetas. "Stop here, stop right here, I'll get out here," I blurted out before the meter hit a fare beyond my means. "I was going to Córcega and Valencia, but looks like I'm out of money," I said, hoping the driver would offer to take me the rest of the way for free.

"You don't say," was all he thought to reply. I handed him the four hundred-peseta coins and climbed out of the car. No doubt there are cab drivers with a heart of gold in this city, but I have no luck: in thirty-four years, I have yet to come across one.

It took me fifteen minutes to limp the three remaining blocks to Elisenda's parents' house. Under normal conditions I would have made it in less than five, but each time I put weight on my right leg, I felt as though someone had pinched the ligaments in my knee with pliers, and I kept having to stop to ease the pain.

When I reached my destination it was seven thirty. I sat down to wait in the doorway of the building across the street and used the time to drink my two remaining cans of beer, which stopped the trembling and unclouded my mind. My misgivings vanished and I felt sure of myself. "There are some formalities that have to be carried out, even if no one requires them," I thought. If I wanted to get out of the boat, first I had to tie up all the loose ends.

When I saw Elisenda leave the building at ten to eight, and saw her yawn and then pause, smiling, to let an old woman by with her shopping bags, I couldn't help feeling a quiver of tenderness run through my body. Suddenly it seemed strange and wonderful that this small, sweet woman had shared three years of her life with me. For a moment I thought I wouldn't have the courage to yell out her name, but before I knew it I was already opening my mouth to call to her. And then Elisenda turned around and scanned the sidewalk across the street to see where that voice shouting her name was coming from. And when she finally saw that it was me, a look of disbelief came over her face, the same look everyone has when they run into someone they know on the street. She must have immediately realized, however, that it was too much of a coincidence for me to be walking by her parents' house at that very moment, so the look of disbelief didn't give way to a smile or the exaggerated display of joy typical of someone who bumps into a friend, but instead to an expression of puzzlement and curiosity, and perhaps to the thought that something terrible had happened and I needed help, because now she saw me cross the street and was no doubt analyzing my appearance and wondering about my limp.

"What's wrong?" she asked, in short, quick breaths as I caught up to her.

"Nothing, nothing's wrong," I reassured her. "I mean, yes, I needed to talk to you for a minute. But there's nothing wrong, Eli, don't worry. How are you?"

"Why are you walking like that?"

"Oh, that . . . It's nothing. Yesterday I was moving some things around at home, and, clumsy me, I hit my knee on the edge of the table."

"My goodness, that's too bad," said Elisenda, forcing a smile. "Well, what is it you need to say? I'm in a bit of a hurry, you know."

In Elisenda's voice I heard a note of contempt, which stung. It didn't do me any good. I sensed she wanted to get rid of me as quickly as possible.

"Right, of course. I'm sure you're in a hurry," I exclaimed, not hiding my irritation. "I should have thought of that earlier. Obviously, it's understandable if you can't spare five minutes for the person you've been living with for the last few years. Totally understandable."

Elisenda looked at me for a minute, apparently surprised by my vulnerability.

"Fine, sorry, you're right," she said, taking a gentler tone. "Look, why don't we get something to eat at the café across the street? It's no big deal if I get to work half an hour late."

That's better, I thought. Still, now that I'd managed to soften her up a bit, I felt even more justified in playing the victim.

"Eat? I just want to talk to you," I said, feigning anger. "Besides, I've already had breakfast. Two vodkas with orange juice, to be exact."

"Is that so?" said Elisenda, looking uncertain whether to take me seriously. "You call that breakfast?"

"Yes, of course. Always. I always have two vodkas with orange juice for breakfast."

"Come on," she said, taking me by the arm, "stop talking nonsense and let's sit down at one of those tables."

We crossed the street and sat down at a table that wasn't very different from the one we were sitting at two weeks ago, when Elisenda ended our relationship. She ordered a café au lait, and I ordered a coffee with Marie Brizard. We said nothing until they brought us the drinks. Then I broke the silence to ask for a cigarette.

Before seeing her I thought I knew exactly what I would say, but now that the moment of truth had arrived, I didn't know where to begin. I felt ridiculous. I'd imagined this encounter as an act of dignity, but the tantrum I'd thrown a few minutes ago ruined any chance of that. Still, I told myself, now there's no going back.

"I imagine you must find all this a little pathetic, and you're probably right, it is pathetic," I said, blowing smoke out of my mouth like a chimney. "Though maybe this is the only way to do these things, maybe honesty is always a little pathetic. After all, there's nothing more pretentious than honesty, don't you think? But there are things that must be said even at the risk of sounding pathetic."

"All right, so what is it you have to say?" asked Elisenda.

"A lot has happened over these past few days that's opened my eyes and freed me from a delusion that lasted for years, a delusion that you, too, were under."

I paused to take a sip of my coffee and cognac, and to glance at her and see if my words had piqued her interest as I hoped. I burned my fingers and set the cup abruptly back down, and I saw that Elisenda was looking at me with real curiosity, eager to hear what I had to say.

"That's why I can't blame you for leaving me," I said slowly. "In fact, I'm the one who feels guilty. For too long I've been wearing a borrowed suit. I fooled everyone, and what's worse, I fooled myself. But all that's in the past now. I've taken off the suit and am now naked." With both hands I gestured to my body, as though trying to show her that I really was naked just then. "And now I understand that sooner or later our relationship had to end. Because you didn't fall in love with a failure, but with someone who had a place in the world. You fell in love with a man who had a career and conventional expectations and ambitions and a future. But that man only seemed to exist, he was a fiction, a fake, a phony. That's why our relationship was doomed to fail. And I had no clue. In fact, now I know you saw it a lot sooner than I did. My god, I've been so blind all these years! I can imagine your disappointment when you started to see who I really was, when you saw I had nothing to do with the person you fell in love with. I can imagine your disappointment when you saw, for instance, how I was failing at my career and didn't realize it, when you saw the clumsy tricks I'd use to hide my lack of strength or courage, my total inability to handle life. But you kept fighting for me, you, too, refused to accept the obvious truth. Like when you tried to get me to take on cases and trials that I felt I couldn't handle, or all those times you hinted at the possibility of having children, moving out of my mom's house, starting a normal, everyday family . . . And I'd change the subject and slink away, and you'd pretend you didn't mind—poor Elisenda. I wonder how you were able to put up with me for so long."

Elisenda shook her head and started to say something.

"No, please, don't interrupt. Let me finish," I said, stopping her with my hand. "You could have accepted that things weren't going well for me, but you couldn't admit that I was someone else, the exact opposite of the person you had known. Yes, I know you think you didn't fall in love with me only for what I was or seemed to be. But you fall in love with who you fall in love with. And it becomes harder and harder to dissociate someone's character from the social and personal context they're embedded in. You thought I was a man of action, a man who could handle life, a lawyer-man who had a specific place in this world. And I wasn't. I failed you. I didn't know how to be who you thought I was."

My mouth was dry and I paused for a moment. I sipped my coffee, still too hot, and took the last drag of the cigarette. My eyes met Elisenda's for a second and I thought I saw a shadow of sadness in them. I looked down and kept talking.

"It was all a sham. I mean, not everything: my love was real, and so were all the happy times we spent together. But a relationship can't be based on only a few happy times. There has to be a common purpose, a single direction. And I couldn't keep up my end of the bargain. I pretended I could, but I couldn't. Because even though I didn't know it, I was sinking, even though I didn't want to admit it, I was drifting irreversibly toward my real destiny. And now that I'm finally here, now that I know where my place is, I feel like a weight has been lifted. And I'm starting to understand everything."

I looked up, but now it was Elisenda who had bowed her

head. Her blond bangs covered her eyes. I wondered if she was hiding a tear.

"While it hurts to lose you," I went on, "I understand why you left me. You had no other way out, and this was the best for both of us. Eventually I would have ended up dragging you down with me, because there's nothing so ruthless or destructive or contagious as a thirst for failure. And that life wasn't for you, just as the life I've been living these past few years wasn't for me. You got out in time, Elisenda. And I'm glad, even if it's painful and hard to accept that I won't see you again. I had to tell you. I wanted you to know that at last I understood your decision."

I sat in silence, watching Elisenda. Her head was still lowered, blond hair still covering her face. And I realized how vulnerable our thoughts are, how malleable and frail words are, even when they're spoken with as much conviction and honesty as I had just mustered. Because as I watched her I realized that, in spite of everything I had said, a single gesture from Elisenda (the motion that raises the barrier blocking the way) would have been enough for me to take back my words. And I must admit that for a few seconds, as she struggled to hide her tears, I left my destiny suspended in midair, and even thought that such a gesture was still possible. But once again I was wrong. It wasn't possible. Fortunately for both of us, it was no longer possible.

When Elisenda at last turned her face to me, I could see the wet streaks of her tears, and a fragile, nervous smile.

"Well . . . I guess now it's been said, right?" she replied, wiping her cheek with the back of her hand.

I knew that she wouldn't say anything else, that she couldn't say anything else. I sat up slightly and motioned for the waiter to bring us the check.

"You'll have to pay," I said, smiling and shrugging. "I haven't got a cent."

After Elisenda paid, we both lit another cigarette and smoked in silence for a few minutes.

"Well, now I really do have to go," she said at last, getting up.

We left the café table and walked together a short ways,

stopping at a traffic light. We gave each other one last kiss good-bye, a shy, hasty kiss on the mouth.

"Where are you headed?" asked Elisenda afterward.

"I'm going home. I still haven't slept."

"I gathered. And how are you going to get home if you haven't got any money?"

"Well, if I can borrow two hundred pesetas I'll catch a bus on Casanova."

Elisenda reached for her bag and looked around inside.

"Here," she said, handing me a thousand-peseta bill and smiling, this time with that sweetness I liked so much, that sweet, luminous smile that managed to arouse in me, at the same time, a desire to protect and to be protected. "You'd better get a taxi. With your leg like that you won't make it to the bus stop."

I thanked her and we parted ways. Elisenda walked up Villarroel, toward the Hospital Clínico. I stood still in the middle of the sidewalk, watching her walk away until her small shape disappeared into the crowd. I couldn't stop tears from welling up in my eyes.

Every passing requires certain formalities, even when it's the passing of a way of life.

Now that the requirements for my relationship with Elisenda had been completed, I had to make my professional death official: I needed to submit the death certificate for my career as a lawyer.

But I didn't want to rush things. That morning, before going back to sleep, I called the office and told the secretary I'd been laid low by a stomach flu and wouldn't be in for a few days. Luisa, accustomed to my absenteeism, merely wished me a speedy recovery.

The next three days I spent shut in at home. I didn't leave even to buy cigarettes: I had some brought to me when I ordered a pizza or Chinese food by phone. I spent many hours in bed. And also in front of the television set. I didn't answer the phone, which rang several times over the course of those three days. I didn't even bother to see if I had any messages on the answering machine.

I was getting ready to take the leap. And I think I wound up enjoying that provisional, transitory state, and even took a certain pleasure in pushing back, day by day, the moment of my definitive break.

On my fourth day of reclusion, however, with the weekend approaching, I decided I couldn't postpone my professional death any longer.

I went to the office at mid-morning and notified Santasusana of my decision to give up practicing law. I was prepared to offer a suitable explanation, to level with him as I had with Elisenda. However—and I think this ultimately disappointed me a little—there was no need. In fact, he didn't even give me the chance to justify my decision. Santasusana received the news calmly, as if he weren't especially surprised, as if somehow he'd been expecting it. He didn't attempt to persuade me to change my mind. Later, when I said good-bye to Luisa, I learned that Maserachs, that bastard, had told Santasusana about the embarrassing episode a few days back in front of the offices of the Bar Association. In any case, I saw that, independently of my shameful and unbecoming behavior over the previous days, Santasusana had been expecting such a decision for quite some time. Once again I was the blindest of all, the last one to know where things were headed.

We said good-bye with an affectionate embrace, and he reiterated that even though we wouldn't be colleagues anymore, I could still count on him for anything I needed. I thanked him, not only for that last show of generosity, but for giving me his trust and respect, even when I had made it clear I didn't deserve them. I left his office, holding back my emotions. In the hallway I realized that, like a fool, I forgot to ask him how everything had turned out with his daughter.

In my office, I gathered only my strictly personal belongings: my planner, a pipe I had never used, three or four crime novels, a leather wallet with a photo of Elisenda inside, some sunglasses, my diploma, and little else. The legal books, and my collection of law compendiums, I decided to leave in the office, even though they had cost me an arm and a leg, since I wasn't going to need them anymore. I was also about to leave behind my laptop—the same computer that for the past few weeks, using the considerable free time I now have on my hands, I've been using to write this story—but at the last minute, not yet knowing what I'd use it for, I decided to take it with me.

I didn't say good-bye to Maserachs. Of course, he wasn't in the office just then, but even if he had been I still wouldn't have said good-bye, not because I was angry he'd told Santasusana about my alcoholic ravings, but so I wouldn't have to see his barely masked glee at my resignation, a resignation he would interpret, I felt certain, as confirmation of his definitive triumph over me.

Luisa walked me to the foyer. "Oh, this is all so sad!" she kept saying softly as I arranged my belongings in the elevator. She didn't cry, but she came pretty close. Standing at the door, she waved her hand slowly while the elevator began to descend. This final image of her made me feel like a teenager about to embark on a long voyage.

That same morning I went to the Bar Association to officially give up my membership. When I completed the paperwork, after two hours going from office to office and from secretary to secretary, I shut myself in the library for five minutes to write a few lines to Marasco. In my letter, cordially but sloppily written, I apologized for missing Tuesday's appointment but added that, since I suddenly had to give up the profession for personal reasons, I assumed that the unfortunate matter with Señora Ruscarons, about which I felt deeply ashamed, had been definitively settled, and that it wouldn't be necessary to schedule a new appointment.

I enclosed the letter in an envelope I fabricated myself out of a blank sheet of paper that the librarian kindly gave to me, and left it for Marasco at the main office.

Then, after completing all the formalities that concluded my career as a lawyer, and moved by that attraction that losers feel to the scenes of their defeats, I took one final stroll through the Bar Association's headquarters.

13

Six months have gone by since that day. I know because I took the trouble to mark the date on the greasy, splotched calendar hanging on my kitchen wall. A little bit ago, on my way to the refrigerator to grab a yogurt, I stood staring at that calendar, perplexed, counting the weeks over and over again to make sure I hadn't made a mistake. I don't know whether it feels like a very long or a very short time, but at any rate I was surprised to see it had been six months.

But then everything surprises me since I changed my life. I'm surprised by the passage of time, and by the fact that concepts like months or days or years exist to measure it. I'm surprised when I look at myself in the mirror and see the same face, with only minor variations, that someone else before me wore in my place; or when I get up in the morning and see the sun streaming in through my bedroom windows, demanding nothing in return; or when I walk into a café and the waiter asks me what I'll have. I'm surprised not to find anxiety where my intuition and instinct, honed over the years, tell me to expect it, and I'm surprised there are places in the world I still haven't seen and never will see, despite the fact that there's life there, and people like me, like all of us. I'm surprised and astonished to be sitting here and living still, and to know that perhaps no one is thinking of me or expecting anything of me, any action, any sign. I'm surprised when I walk down the street and discover I'm still a part of this city, when I remember that Elisenda still lives here, though I no longer see her or run into her, when nightfall catches me wandering aimlessly through a distant, unfamiliar neighborhood. Everything surprises and astonishes me and leaves me perplexed, the smallest things as well as the most arcane questions my mind can imagine. I know it won't always be this way, because the surprise and novelty will eventually wear off, and I'll adjust to this new order which my eyes and nose and hands and memory are slowly discovering. But I'll enjoy this state of grace as long as it lasts. And I know I can be certain that even when I grow tired of all this, and melancholy finally gets the better of me, I'll at least have the consolation and the peace of mind of knowing I don't have to fight other people's battles, battles I wasn't cut out for and would be destined to lose.

As far as everything else goes, I float through my days and don't wonder where they'll take me. I'm not worried about the future. Not even about my survival. The fact is, things are working out for me at the moment, and I get by. And I don't see any reason things won't continue like this.

Though it may sound odd, I now work in the theater. Who would have guessed? Alberto spoke to his friend Óscar Music, who offered me a walk-on part in his latest play. At one point in the show, I cross the stage carrying a cardboard dresser. My appearance is somewhat superfluous, and I suspect Óscar Music inserted it into the script solely to justify the thirty-five hundred pesetas he pays me each night, but I'm in no position to refuse anyone's generosity. Incidentally, my mother saw the show without telling me and came away extremely disappointed. To ease her distress at the news that I'd broken up with Elisenda and stopped practicing law, I had slightly exaggerated my character's importance in the play. The poor thing spent the whole two hours looking for me and in the end could only make out a lock of hair sticking out above the dresser I lugged across the stage. It was such a letdown that she couldn't bring herself to say she had seen the show until two weeks later, at the airport, just before she got on the plane back to Madrid. "Well, you've got to start somewhere," she said at last, when she saw I was blushing.

Once in a while, after the show, Alberto meets me outside the theater door and takes me out for dinner and drinks. We haven't spoken about his family's financial situation again, but I'm starting to think the tale of imminent ruin was just one of his inventions, a ruse to avoid always making excuses for living such a comfortable life. Either way, he's still the same. And he'll stay the same. Continuing his descent toward the same point where I, too, a few steps behind him, am headed. Once again Alberto is my guide. Once again he's the leader and I'm just a follower. But now I know he's leading me down the right path.

There's nothing to be afraid of. Fear and anxiety and guilt have vanished. I'll continue to live in this world until I have to leave it. As will everyone: those who made it big and those who didn't, those who became someone in this life and those who didn't, those who did important and productive things and those who did nothing, those who were loved and those who couldn't manage to make somebody love them, those who lived and those who didn't know how. Sooner or later everyone disappears from this story, and in the end hardly anything will be left of anyone.

I'm just one more in the crowd. One of those little dots you see as you fly over the city in an airplane. I'm still alive. And that's enough. Contrary to what you might think, it's easier to survive when you lack ambition. Death comes sooner for those who strike out through the jungle looking for a way out than for those who await their end under the shade of a palm tree, not caring what they'll eat the next day. That's how I live now. And I enjoy my purposeless waiting. Future? I don't even really know what that means.

In a little while I'll turn off this computer and go to the theater to earn my charity handout. I know that Óscar Music's play, which is called *Sweat* and is about the hardships of housewives, won't run indefinitely. But there may be other plays after this one, and I may still be able to abuse my friends' generosity. And if not, I'll find something. Anything, it doesn't matter what. Or perhaps I can go back to Sant Honorat and ask Ernest (beg him if need be) to take me on at the hotel, perhaps to fill that bellhop position which everyone turns down, and which he might still need someone to cover.